RETALIATION

RETALIATION

BORIS CHRONICLES™ BOOK TWO

PAUL C. MIDDLETON

MICHAEL ANDERLE

DISRUPTIVE IMAGINATION

LMBPN Publishing
PMB 196, 2540 South Maryland Pkwy
Las Vegas, NV 89109

First US edition, 2016
Version 1.04, December 2020
Print ISBN: 978-1-64202-960-4

CHAPTER ONE

Command Bunker West of Romanovka

Boris was tired. But the good tired. The battle would take place tomorrow. His raiders had continued to mark the progress of the NVG column. The enemy column was continuing to travel, beyond all common sense, along the original route. Without his force blocking them, the NVG would catch the refugees around the time they were forced to leave the highway. His men were dug in and prepared. Eighty Weres positioned on either end of the planned ambush site. In place to cut off any retreat or hard push forward. As soon as scouting confirmed the NVG route once more, those at the alternate ambush site would move to join the main force.

Boris had given Danislav command of the secondary site forces. Primary tasking for them was the reinforcement of the left flank of the primary group and sealing off the ends of the ambush against any NVG forces trying to escape. He had positioned two-thirds of his men on the right flank. If the enemy detected re-enforcements early, there would be no simple place to break through his lines.

It was an Insurance plan. The less that could be confirmed about his force, the more damage he could do to the NVG for the fewest losses.

Central to the plan was the strategy to take out the vehicles. Those at the front of the column would be attacked first, then any at the rear. Second priority would be the armor. The most dangerous vehicle that the NVG had were agile APCs, so the lighter shoulder-mounted launchers, the Carl Gustavs, were to be used against them. Other tanks or reinforced vehicles could then be picked off by anti-tank missiles.

A group of twenty snipers had established firing positions and chose range markers at each site. Fighters, mostly drawn from the mercenaries with a few hunters in the mix, had been given half the stockpile of Barret M82 guns, shoulder-fired semi-automatic rifles. The large .50 caliber weapons had the balance of long range and high stopping power that this type of battle required.

All the marksmen had orders to disable and destroy any truck that tried to circle the battle for strategic position or attempt to run. Boris wanted no one to escape, especially in a highly mobile vehicle.

The anger of his men and his own need for retribution demanded that this engagement be a mighty blow. Retaliation for the deaths of his people. A justified response to their betrayal by their government. In a pinch, he could win against the approaching force with the troops already in place, but doing so without the reinforcements from the alternate site risked higher casualties.

While Boris wanted to win this battle, he had to achieve victory in his war. Sacrificing his forces at this point in the campaign would endanger everything they sought to preserve.

ADAM had confirmed that the two companies of NVG had orders to run the refugees to ground. The command included capturing as many refugees as possible., they would march the prisoners to a position greater than a hundred and fifty miles north of their home in Romanovka.

Boris had marked the location and was deciding whether or not to investigate the region once the battle was finished. The NVG had selected it for a reason. It was not convenient for a transport depot, or the exchange of prisoners.

Paul came running in. "Boss, we have confirmation. The NVG is heading for the primary route. The raiders will move to their areas of responsibility now. Danislav has Weres shadowing them. A relay of wolf howls if they divert from what we know of their routes." Paul grimaced. "It seems so... old school to be effectively yelling signals for communications. What are we? Tribesmen?"

Boris grinned. "Ahh, but the pack can recognize each other's howls, while it will be just usual sounds to the NVG. How are additional wolf howls unusual in the wilderness? They may have some signal detectors. Remove the need for electronic transmissions, and they will think whoever was ambushing them gave up. Human forces wouldn't be using wolf howls now, would they?" His grin turned his face to an expression of vicious anticipation and glee.

Janna shook her head. "It is not like these troops are professionals, Boris. Oh, some probably are, no doubt. But the bulk are street thugs given a veneer of training and thrown into uniform." A look of disgust covered her face, and she spat on the ground. "I doubt that your risk estimates are close. I'd be surprised if they cause half the damage you are expecting."

Boris shrugged "Better to be prepared for the worst. My greatest regret is running the operation from a bunker in the rear. I never liked leading from the back. Besides, it is vital we eliminate this group. Its orders are not kind to our people. Once the threat they represent is gone, we can focus more on finding information that will help us decide what to do next."

Janna looked at him in a combination of consideration and buried anger. "With Bethany Anne willing to extract them, the fifteen agents I can still contact are ready to look for that information. As an Englishman might put it 'Something is rotten in the kingdom of Denmark,' yes? They are patriots, wanting to look after their country even though it has abandoned them."

She continued, "I have not told them about what forces will use that knowledge. One or two of them may put the bits and pieces together, but it is not important. I hand-picked all of these people. They trust me as I trust them."

A sour look appeared on her face. "We were betrayed, and I now know by whom. I never wanted Sergeant Brogonovich on my team, but he was assigned by someone above my Colonel's pay grade. A plant from the start, it seems. I hope I get to see him on his knees, begging for his life, before I shoot him in the back of his worthless head."

Boris grinned. At least she had the penalties for fuckups and traitors in her current world down pat. Didn't seem squeamish about it either. It showed a proper perspective on the realities of their situation. He just wished that it did not make her even more attractive.

Dragging his mind back to the conversation, he said, "Now you two, we have a busy day tomorrow. Go, get some sleep." Boris waved toward the exit of their half-buried command post.

Lance had given their command and control groups enough radios for officers and senior non-coms, so they really could take advantage of someone giving orders from the rear. Boris was the only person with the experience and the knowledge of their other assets, so he was forced into a more protected position, although it continued to rankle him.

A dozen or more cameras had been linked into a network designed by TOM and coordinated by ADAM to enable Boris to come as close as possible to the action while still strategically overseeing the battle. It was a compact and comprehensive setup, with an added benefit that everything could be moved into the shipping container/command transport once the fight was over.

Paul responded, "After you, boss."

Boris shook his head, "You know I never sleep before an op. I'll go for a walk among the troops, making sure they know I trust them to do their jobs. Boost their confidence, boost their morale. Show I care for them."

Janna glanced questioningly at Paul who answered the unasked question, "He does this every time. No matter the size or scope of the mission. Anything from a squad op to company-sized. The night before the battle he won't sleep. Not that it seems to affect his ability to do the job well. Just makes me, a mere mortal, kinda jealous. Gets me every time he does that, too." He shook his head and headed tiredly to his sleeping bag.

Watching Paul leave, Boris raised an eyebrow at Janna, who shrugged and headed out. He was finding her less distracting to work with now, the passage of time allowing him to re-associate her smell. He couldn't help but admire the grace with which she walked and the sway of her assets as she left. Internally he found himself wrestling with a dilemma. She was not an option for romance. No good commander could seek amorous entanglements with operational subordinates. But he was undeniably attracted to her.

He headed out to circulate among the troops. It was a cold camp tonight, with no fires, but hopefully, he could hearten them. Boris still wished he could fight with them and swore to himself that next time he would not be kept out of the action.

CHAPTER TWO

Ambush site west of Romanovka, Siberia

When morning broke, there was a mist of rain. Perfect weather for ducks and an ambush. Boris was talking to his field officers. They were expecting the NVG force from the West to arrive in three hours, so he had time to conference with them and send them back to their men. The other ambush force had moved to within a mile last night from their positions to the northeast of the route that the NVG had chosen. They would belly crawl into position over the next three hours.

These reinforcements would be in position and had orders to advance fast on the initiation of combat. It would be a quick, ugly fight. They couldn't risk whoever was sent to investigate realizing how many men were involved. Danislav was grumpy, though. He wouldn't be going wolf with the rest of the pack.

Boris needed him and his experience to command the other flank and as the backup commander.

Morale was high. Now they had to wait, and Boris

prayed that everyone stuck to the plan. He had enough men and Weres to chase down anyone fleeing from a botched ambush, but it would increase his casualties. He needed a complete success, not a partial one. Any perceived failures would make future actions... harder.

Boris spoke, "We must stick to the opening moves of the plan. Impress the importance of surprise on your men. It will reduce our casualties immensely. After confusion has spread through their ranks, any deviation from the plan for advantage once the battle is joined, fine. But stick to taking out their APCs and a vehicle at both the front and rear of the column first. No rifle fire before we hear the Carl Gustavs hit."

The officers nodded, and he dismissed them.

They heard the column approaching about five minutes before they were in the center of the trap. When the surveillance system showed the column in position, Boris clicked the radio four times, giving the Carl Gustav teams weapons-free status. The smells of propellant, explosives, burning metal and flesh soon filled the air. Screams of agony came from the men in the APCs as they burst into flames, their fuel tanks ruptured. The destruction could be heard for miles. The explosions signaled the ambushing riflemen to open fire on the column from both sides.

With the road blocked at both ends by burning APCs, the NVG troops quickly disembarked. It was that or risk certain death inside their vehicles once the Carl Gustavs were re-loaded. The NVG troops threw themselves into the ditches at the edges of the roadway. They scrambled to return fire. Boris could hear an increase in weapon reports from the other side of the ambush as his reserves flooded into the fight on that flank.

This battle was going far smoother than he could have imagined.

Boris gave orders over the radio, directing troops to concentrate their fire on the more substantial concentrations of enemies he could see through the video feeds.

Suddenly an explosion rocked his half-buried command post. He felt a chunk of the wood from the wall slam into his chest as he was thrown backwards with his chair. Then all he knew was darkness.

Danislav swore when he saw the explosion near the command post and heard a burst of static over the radio. Orders from Boris stopped transmitting. "Fuck your mothers you black asses" could be heard for some distance as he got himself under control.

"Bear one, do you copy? Bear One, Two or Three, if any of you copy, please respond."

There was silence over the radio.

"This is Wolf One. Communications with Bears has been terminated. Wolf One is now taking command and control until communications are re-established."

"Cossack Alpha and Cossack Zeta move to cut the ends of the roads NOW. Nova troops are moving to escape the Bear trap."

Confirmations filtered back from all six in command of the companies and platoons so designated and Danislav saw soldiers swarming to cut off the ends of the ambush site.

"Valkyrie Alpha One, break half a squad from your group off and send it to bunker Bear and see what happened. Re-establish communications if possible."

Confirmation came across. They were too far away for Danislav to see any movement but the Valkyrie groups comprised a mix of mercenaries with medic training and those doctors and nurses who chose to stay. If anything could be done, they would do it.

As new knots of resistance formed Danislav redirected fire at them. The occasional shot from the Carl Gustavs could be heard being fired into the NVG holdouts now as covering fire kept the heads of those in the ditches down.

Danislav prayed that whatever had hit had just knocked out the radios in the command bunker. He certainly did not want to inherit control of the entire operation. He would do it, but it was not something he wanted. Boris had raised him from a pup when he found Danislav in an orphanage in the north. He did not want to be mourning the only real father he had known. But, if it came to that, he would carry on his goals and mission.

A familiar voice crackled over the radio. Dan's. "Wolf One, this is Skyhawk. Do you request air support? Four armed pods are available and less than a minute out." Boris had discussed this with him in detail. Under no circumstances was he to call in air support unless the ambush failed. It hadn't.

"Negative Skyhawk. Negative. Ambush is stable. Air support is not required. Keep Ace out at this time."

"It would reduce casualties Wolf One."

"Using it as this juncture may increase all future casualties Skyhawk. Do not engage Skyhawk. Please clear the line."

Danislav sweated profusely after he signed off. He hoped he hadn't pissed Bethany Anne's team off. There was no way he wanted to do that. However, he also needed to stick to that part of the plan. He hoped they understood 'man on-site' situations. Dan had apparently wanted to get the air support down there. What a proklyatyy klastera yebat he thought.

Taking a deep breath, he turned back to commanding the battle. The last thing he wanted was to give them a bigger excuse to be angry. He was sure he wouldn't like it if he made her team angry.

Janna returned to consciousness with the sting of long cuts up and down her arms, as well as many nicks and light wounds with plastic shrapnel in them. They were all surface wounds, though. She slowly and carefully looked around. The entire setup was trashed. There was no way they could command from here, so she turned to the exit. It was blocked, with the framing timbers fallen into haphazard piles.

"Boris, if you're gonna command the rest of this, you need to get out of here."

There was silence.

Janna looked around and saw Paul on the ground, but breathing. He was probably unconscious. As she turned further, she saw Boris. He was still in his chair but didn't seem to be moving. As her vision cleared more, she realized that he looked as if he were pinned to the seat by a three-foot splinter of wood that went through his chest. It was the only way he and the chair could still be together.

Her basic training kicked in. He was the priority casualty if still alive. She moved over to him and checked his pulse. It was weak and thready, but present. Turning him and the chair, so he was on his side, she found that her initial guess was correct. There was a piece of wood penetrating the back of the seat. She quickly looked around the bunker for the first aid kit, but could not see the familiar red cross of its cover. The equipment was probably somewhere under chunks of wood or beneath some of the dirt that had rolled in. She didn't have time to look for it, let alone dig it out.

She swore. Then she thought about the situation. She had to get the damned splinter off the seat and out of Boris. She was surprised. Blood had pooled under him, but not as much as she expected. The fragment must be sealing the wound.

She started by twisting the chair back and forth around the splinter. It had gone in low on Boris's chest. It had missed the heart and, although it was beating steadily, she couldn't see any signs of consciousness nor breathing. She twisted the chair back and forth trying to loosen it. She heard the wood whine as she applied gentle pressure. Finally, it broke free. Unfortunately, a fair chunk of the splinter through Boris's back came loose as well, and his blood pumped out quickly. She swore in dismay and ripped off her BDU shirt to help put pressure on the wound.

Pressing the shirt tightly against the gushing wound, she now had his blood covering much of her body, trickling into many of her injuries. Something in the back of her mind tickled at her. She tried to place it. Then it clicked. Bethany Anne had mentioned that she had healed a massive bullet wound all the way through her body some time ago. She had said it had taken a lot of energy but that she had been 'weaker' back then. Standard first aid practice was to leave an object like this in the wound, but Boris was far older than Bethany Anne. Surely his body had access to whatever energy Bethany Anne had referred to after all that time.

She knew the legends all referred to how fast werewolves healed, and the wolves were scared of Boris. That meant he recovered at a similar rate or a group of them would have taken him out. She had a minute of indecision before checking his pulse. It was getting weaker. If the splinter was left in, she felt he would die. Taking it out, with his presumably faster healing, might be his best chance. It was then she noticed that her shirt wasn't soaked through yet. It should have been with the amount of blood that had been coming out. That clinched it for her.

She quickly moved him from the chair and rolled him onto his back. Bracing one foot on his chest next to the splinter and the other on the floor beside his body, she grabbed it above where the blood was on the log fragment. She pulled hard, trying to keep it coming out as straight as possible. As she was pulling it out, Janna could feel her feet slipping. She fell forward when it came out more easily than she had expected. Her face intersected with the small geyser of blood spraying from his chest wound.

Startled, she gasped as she landed, swallowing a fair amount of blood in the process. Rolling away from the wound, she grabbed the BDU top again to put pressure back on the injury. She felt somewhat queasy at having swallowed human (well, Werebear) blood but continued to keep the pressure on for a minute. When she pulled the fabric away, there was a thick scab over the area, so she checked his pulse again. It was stronger than the last time she felt for it.

But he still wasn't breathing.

She switched to rescue breathing, alternating with light compressions to his chest. As she was taking a breath in over his mouth, he coughed a wet fountain of blood into her face. By reflex, she swallowed more of the blood, not even spluttering as she had earlier. He started breathing well on his own. She let out a relieved sigh.

The sounds of combat had died down outside, either while she was unconscious or while she had been treating Boris. She looked down at her body. She was covered from head to toe in blood, mostly his. Her vision blurred as she looked back up at Boris's face. He was quite handsome, she thought vaguely. Then it occurred to her that shock must be kicking in. Why else would she think that about her commanding officer? She looked up at his eyes, saw them opening, and murmured "Such wonderful eyes, my beautiful…" as she collapsed over him.

As Boris regained consciousness, he looked down his body at the person who had, from the look of the blood on their face, been giving him first aid. He heard a ragged feminine voice say "Such wonderful eyes, my beautiful..." and felt her collapse on him. He couldn't recognize her by looks, as covered in blood as she was. So much it masked her odor. He could tell it was a 'she' when the person collapsed on him. He checked her pulse. It was strong and steady. He shook his head to clear it and realized three things.

Wreckage filled the bunker. The damage was severe enough all the equipment would be a write-off.

From the sounds of things, the battle was over. As he doubted he had been out for long, he felt the most likely reason was that they had one convincing victory.

And finally, the bunker was partially collapsed in on itself. There was no exit. The woman who had collapsed on him had to be Janna. His mind fought to think clearly. Had Janna called him 'My beautiful...'?

Boris spent several moments as he tried to get his mind wrapped around her comment.

Had they both been hiding their attraction from the other? Was it just shock that had caused her to say that? How could he deny the lure towards her now? How could they work together now? These were amongst the questions that rocketed through his mind. It wasn't like he could answer them right now so he shook himself and refocused on the problems that he could address.

While his mind kept whirling, he moved the only two tables left intact into a shelter for Paul and Janna. The blood on the floor, the disarray of the room in general and the position of the chair in which he had been sitting told him what the extent of his injuries must have been.

He saw the massive splinter of wood and winced internally. With him unconscious and that chunk through his body, Janna may have saved his life by her actions. Impaling was one of the few things that Weres couldn't necessarily deal with for more than a couple of hours. When the body couldn't expel the object, healing of the damage stopped.

Janna was either incredibly smart and willing to take risks, or foolhardy. Boris didn't believe the reckless option. That opinion was further validated when he found her blood-soaked BDU top. Rather than waste time digging out the first aid kit from a shattered section of the bunker she had used materials at hand to put pressure on his wound.

He carefully moved Paul and Janna's unconscious bodies to a protected position under the tables, then looked for the best exit strategy. Shifting the timbers away from the door seemed to be a bad idea. He couldn't be sure that moving debris out of the jumble would not cause more of the bunker to collapse, so he looked for the area that had the most blast damage.

He undressed, and put his clothes under Janna's head as a cushion, trying very hard not to examine his caring action. He changed to his bear form and dug a way out. The combination of his strength and the sharp claws of his bear meant that it didn't take him long. The timbers in that area had shattered, and the bunker hadn't been thoroughly dug in to start. Instead, they'd covered the upper section in dirt and hid it in turf to camouflage it as a small hillock.

He dug carefully, compressing the sides and roof of the tunnel with his body as he moved forward. When the excavation broke through to the surface (well, into the crater that had to be the cause of the problem at least), he found a small group of four had unpacked their collapsible shovels and were beginning to dig to meet him. Three backboards were lying on the edge of the crater with one of the Valkyrie nurses and one of the merc medics organizing supplies. Those manning the shovels took a quick step back.

Boris quickly moved over to the backboards and touched two of them. He then pointed to the rope on one of the soldiers webbing and indicated they should tie the backboards to him. When the nurse objected, the merc medic overruled her. Dragging the backboards behind him, secured to his waist, Boris lumbered back down the tunnel. He stopped every few steps to compress the sides and top again, trying to ensure that their escape route would remain safe. Once all the way back, Boris changed back to his human form. Moving over to his unconscious subordinates, he checked their status. Both had steady pulses and were breathing well. He got dressed before he carefully strapped Paul and Janna to the backboards.

He tied Paul's backboard to the rope at his waist. Crouching down to avoid the tunnel ceiling, he pulled Janna on the backboard with him, spooling out the waist rope. As soon as he cleared Janna and backboard from the tunnel he passed her off to the medics and then helped the four waiting soldiers pull Paul up the shaft on the backboard sled with the rope.

He decided it was best not to dwell on their injuries. The medic and the nurse declared them both stable, and he had troops to organize. They had to leave in the next six hours for their deployment areas. As it stood, no one would be able to pinpoint the time this battle had taken place, and he wanted to maintain the secrecy as long as possible. The sooner his teams could gather information, the sooner he would have more targets to strike.

The first step to retaliation was complete.

CHAPTER THREE

Unknown location in Russia

Shen was terrified of the vampire that had captured him.

What had been a profitable deal for the family's export business had gone well. His personal arrangement had gone horribly wrong.

The person with whom he was dealing had turned out to be a vampire. Too late, he'd smelt the rotting blood odor as he entered the meeting. He had tried to flee, but the vampire had covered all the exits with his men. Not wanting to risk exposure by changing in the middle of a city, bringing worse on himself, had seemed the best strategy. Even if it led to him being captured.

He'd been wrong. Any death, no matter how painful would have been better than the last two? Or was it three, months of captivity, of being used as a blood source for the monster to try to *improve* his human lieutenants. Most of them had wasted away within a week. Their corpses were used to supplement his food. One, the volunteer of two subjects ago, Andrev he had been called, had changed.

Shen's family wouldn't even be looking for him yet. They would assume he was working on more of his private deals. They'd never approved of his black market dealings.

He had been trapped by the rumor of some experimental processors that never really existed. In exchange, he would provide the location of a hidden weapon dump from the fall of the Soviet Union he had discovered. His curiosity had led him to that arms dump as inevitably as it had into this trap.

Now he was in a cage, a blood bank for this madman's experiments. He knew his family was unusual. The previous werecat attempts to change others were rarely successful. Before the fortunate turn of the Russian, Andrev, he would have rated them as rumor alone.

He prayed that he would soon be allowed to die. He didn't think it likely, though. The vampire still had a use for him. Or at least his blood.

CHAPTER FOUR

Command Container, Wilderness, Siberia

Boris was agitated. It had been three days since the battle. Janna had remained unconscious. Due to the necessity of destroying the equipment that couldn't be salvaged from the bunker, it had been a full day before they'd been able to meet up with the container. She remained unconscious. This limbo, especially after what she said, was worse than his headaches. Each day had dragged like a year of headaches.

The secure phone rang, the ID indicating Frank. He hit the button and answered gruffly, "Boris."

"Hey, it's Frank, Boris. Lance and Dan were concerned that the strike on your bunker might indicate that someone had figured a way to trace our communications, so we went back over the first half of the battle. We had footage from three angles of the shot that hit the bunker. The vehicle was the lead, and the turret had been knocked askew by the initial strike. It looks like they already had a round up the spout and it cooked off."

There was a frown in his voice for the next discussion. "The crater and damage were not consistent with the standard HE round, though. Looks like the Russians, or at least the NVG, have cooked up something new. Something more powerful. Be careful. There may be some other Weres or even vampires on their side, too. I'm getting rumblings that the head of this NVG group is different. Different enough that none of my contacts were willing or able to sell information to European or American foreign intel about the group. The only reason I got anything was that I already knew their name. Even then it cost me a favor. One I need your help with."

Frank continued, "I need you to take out a facility for the favor. Best to keep our accounts current. Besides, they said this one would put them in our debt. Apparently, an NVG linked company has taken over security for one of the Siberian oil refineries. Now production is officially down fifteen percent. The ministry my contact works for has proof that they are siphoning that fuel into their supply lines, but Defense and the other government departments are refusing to act. He wants it stopped, with no indication of outside help. Dan is biting at the bit and wants to come."

Boris sighed. It would be good to go and cause some mayhem, but that would leave either Danislav or Paul in charge. Danislav, he thought with a frown. Paul was just too oddball. "If Janna were operational, I'd say certainly, Frank. Between her, Danislav and Paul they could do anything that was needed while I was away. But she is not up. I am getting worried. She is losing weight despite being on a nutrient IV. I would guess nine or so kilograms over the last two days. If some..." He cut himself off.

He wasn't going to admit that if something went wrong if she died, he wanted to be next to her. The confusion of his emotions made it difficult for him to sort things out. Somehow, his failure to be with his last love when she died and the situation with Janna had become entwined. He had no idea why or when that had happened.

There was a loud sigh over the line. "Boris, Why didn't you mention the weight drop earlier? Dan will come down to pick you up. A spare pod will take Janna to Bethany Anne. Dan needs some time out of the office anyway. You and Dan will head straight to the refinery. We'll get Janna into the medical pod and get her better. Capiche? Bethany Anne is gonna be pissed at you, again. The only reason you haven't gotten a visit for the bunker incident is it was probably bad luck. Oh, we are keeping a pod loaded with sintered metal/silver ammo on standby for your first op. With other Weres in the opposition, your guys might need it, and there's space for it in that container."

Boris slumped a little, partly in relief and partly in shame. Both offers of help were something he should have considered. "Yes, Frank." His voice was a little disconsolate. Then he perked up "But the refinery, we are just taking out their security right? Not the plant operators?"

"Of course. Bethany Anne wouldn't consider any other way. Be ready in an hour. It'll take me that long to find a medic to put in the pod with Janna."

CHAPTER FIVE

The Command Container, Russia

Frank was as good as his word. Exactly an hour later two pods landed, and Dan stepped out of the first. One of the Queen Bitch's Elite stepped out of the other and helped Boris secure Janna in the pod. They placed the banana bag, as Paul insisted on calling the nutrient IV packs, on a hook in the pod cabin. Apparently, the need for evacuation by pod had been considered. He appreciated the help and care the man took. He bowed to him in the traditional Japanese style of showing respect before the Pod left.

Boris quickly went to the doorway and grabbed his web gear and weapons. The body armor was reasonable after his recent bad luck. Dan was a bit surprised to see the mix of weapons Boris was carrying. A silenced MP5 and the pair of silenced Glocks he'd expected. The AA-12 was not on the list of 'discrete' weapons. The short sword instead of a knife or dagger made some sense but was an unusual choice, to say the least. He recognized a pouch for throwing knives as well, and Boris handed him another one. Dan shrugged. He wasn't skilled with throwing knives, but he could hum the tune.

"What do you want to take that for?" Dan asked, indicating the assault shotgun.

Boris gave him the ghost of a smile and answered "It is for two reasons. I have some silver buckshot in case there are Weres among the NVG. There is no real quiet way to take out a Were. Also as TARFU insurance da? Better to have it and not need it…"

Dan grunted in agreement. After so much time hunting down Nosferatu, he wouldn't say it was overkill. Personally, he hoped that things didn't even reach SNAFU levels, but with so many unknowns it was better to be sure. His weapons included a silenced pistol and MP5.

Tonight should be fun, even if it weren't the right time to use the railgun. He deserved a night out like John, and the team had post-Colorado. He hadn't been able to join that evening.

Damn the luck.

Neither of them knew about the other two pods Bethany had on standby, just in case this favor was a trap.

The two landed about a mile away from the refinery and approached it on foot. Despite the dry weather, Boris was wearing a forest camouflage poncho over his equipment. On the approach to the installation, located a couple of miles from any sizable town, there was a pair of bunkers.

Boris raised his hand. Upwind from the bunker, he smelt one of the particularly cheap and vile cigarettes as it was being smoked. Leaving Dan behind, he slipped silently through the scrub.

Dan was close enough, with his improved vision, to see the knife flash and sink to the hilt in the guard's neck. When he caught up with Boris, still removing the blade, he saw that it had gone through the spine and continued through vertebrae. There was a slight grating between metal and bone as the knife was pulled free.

That was a lot of force.

Boris signaled for Dan to head toward the closest bunker from the rear and loped off towards the other one. Their goal here was to make it easier for ADAM to hijack the comms. Dan had a peculiar device that he could plug into whatever system the NVG group was using to give ADAM easy access. He just hoped he was going for the right bunker.

As Dan approached the entrance of his target, a small group of three military-style trucks pulled up. He heard the door handle as it moved and ducked around the side, hiding in the shadows. Boris softly cursed, but Dan focused on the conversation. His Russian wasn't great, but he could get the gist of the conversation. The NVG had sent in a platoon to take over the refinery to secure fuel for their operations.

The action had hit a problem. Events were not at 'it's a trap' level yet, though. As far as Dan was concerned, it was merely more enemies to take out. Boris seemed aggravated by something, though.

Then the wind shifted, and Dan caught the scent of werewolves. Things were fast heading towards needing TARFU insurance. Dan was glad he had a half dozen of the sintered metal/silver magazines for the MP5. It would make things simpler.

The conversation stopped, and the trucks rumbled into the base. After the sound of their passage faded, Dan approached the bunker door again, with his Glock drawn. He kicked up his speed as he entered the room. Within three seconds the four inside were dead. One bullet to the heart and two to the head for each put them down, permanently. The stink of voided bowels filled the air, but he didn't let it bother him.

Taking a deep breath in reaction, he realized that it was strange that the Weres hadn't alerted to Boris. Dan might smell like a normal human, but Boris was another matter.

Dan shook his head, refocused on his primary objective, and plugged one of the connections on the device he had been given into the computer system. At least he had the right bunker for that. Then Boris's voice came quietly over the radio.

"Plans need to change. I need to capture at least one of the Weres alive. We need to know if they are lone wolves or if a pack has joined this insanity. Rush them before they have a chance to spread out to the edges, because if one of them gets away, we may be in trouble."

Dan thought about it for a moment. "Confirmed."

They approached the gate, and Boris started taking off his webbing and pants. He divested himself of the MP5 and Glocks, tucking them behind a rock. He kept on the body armor, though.

"Angle your attack to come in from the left, da? I will try and herd them towards you. They will definitely notice me when I enter." Boris still had the AA12 and had hung four drum magazines from the body armor. "I will change to Pricolici before I charge."

"You can use that," he pointed to the shotgun, "in your other form?" Dan asked

Boris showed him the trigger mechanism. It was about three times larger than the standard size, as was the magazine release. Dan grunted. It was evident over his years Boris had put a lot of thought into things. He probably had more control over his beast-man form than the others too. He somehow couldn't see Peter using a gun in this way.

"I will give you two minutes to get into position. I hope the guards from the perimeter come in when the ruckus starts, so watch your back." Boris's eyes were practically glowing at this point.

Dan headed off to take his position. He heard the soft ripping of cloth as he left. Boris was going all out on this one, that was for sure.

Almost exactly two minutes later Boris headed into the refinery. Thankfully, all of the distilling equipment was well away from the entrance area, no doubt as a safety measure. This area was mostly offices and housing. There was only the slightest hint of petrol in the air. It would be relatively safe for him to use the shotgun. That also meant it would be safe for the NVG to use their weapons, however. He was glad Alecta had designed and made this body armor for him. It had elastic sections between the plates, so it still covered significant portions of his body when he changed.

He heard a shout from near the trucks. He had been seen. Letting loose a bellow he charged in. His first drum held lead shells. The other four, attached to the body armor, were loaded with silver buckshot.

Bullets from their AK74 carbines started cracking around him. He felt several hit his armor, and one grazed his arm. No silver, though. He reached about fifty yards from them and took cover behind a tree.

Aiming, he started firing shots off at those who had their weapons out and firing. Ten had scattered and rushed for cover but were not shooting back at him.

Probably the wolves.

He fired shots at those firing at him. The AA12 wasn't the most accurate weapon, so he was gentle on the trigger, trying for single shots. The range was low, but he wanted to herd them in a direction, not try and kill them where they stood. He managed to take down fourteen of the soldiers in the process, even without trying.

Picking his targets from those on the edges caused them to bunch up without thinking. With the drum on his shotgun empty, he slung it out of the way before charging across the meters between them, now in an arc in front of him, with only his claws and teeth.

They tried to scatter as he advanced but he was too quick. Disemboweling one with a swipe of his paws, he switched to the short sword to take the heads of two more. Dan hadn't asked him about the large grip. He reached his head down and bit a large chunk off another victim's shoulder, severing the arm at the same time. He chewed and swallowed while staring at the others, blood dripping down his jaws and the stringy flesh hanging from between his teeth.

One of the remaining two fainted, accompanied by the stink of hot urine and the sulfurous odor of loaded pants. The final one chose defiance and emptied his magazine into Boris. The response was not what the shooter expected when Boris threw the sword impaling him through the spine. Collapsing after the futile resistance, the soldier's legs stopped working, and he dropped, his weapon wrenched from his grip. Boris kicked him 'lightly' in the head, knocking him unconscious before the bearman knelt and pulled the sword free.

Perhaps they could get information from these two.

Off somewhere to the right, Boris heard bursts of fire and the faintest of sounds that had to be Dan returning fire with his silenced MP5. It appeared to be a substantial group shooting at Dan, armed with something similar to a dozen AK-47s. At least Dan was having some fun, even as the perimeter guards were circling, to get to the target they thought vulnerable. The soldiers were undoubtedly in for a shock.

Boris felt the sting of a half dozen wounds dotted across his limbs as his body ejected a couple of bullets.

He lifted the trucks onto their sides, leaving their wheels impotently spinning, then stalked toward the other vehicles in the lot. The scent of wolf permeated the air, as did the odor of fear. As Boris strode forward, he roared "Therree is noo esscappe. Fight me or die like the currrs you are! Iiif youuu rrrun I will hunt dowwn annny you carrre for!"

There was a moment of silence in which he ejected the drum from the AA12 and, with a little fumbling due to his form, loaded the next one into the gun.

He heard a sudden howl and knew what would come next. He'd taken out large groups of wolves before and knew that their battles followed repeated forms. He knelt and held down the trigger spraying a one hundred eighty degree arc with silver buckshot. He heard a whine with each hit. Six whines, six hits. As he let the shotgun drop onto its sling, two wolves jumped for his neck. He swayed to the side and grabbed one by the scruff of the neck, adding to its momentum as he slammed its head into the other wolf's skull. There was the sickening crunch of snapping and shattering bones.

One of the two remaining wolves circled around him and fled in Dan's direction as the other, braver one, turned in the opposite route. Boris grinned as he made a leap for this last one and with a smack from the hilt of his sword, knocked it unconscious. For good measure, Boris broke all four of the wolf's legs. He wanted information and needed to find out who they were, why would they help the NVG, and who was involved.

He went to check on the remaining wolves, the ones hit by silver. Two were obviously dead. The other four were severely injured, although one was trying to crawl away. Boris broke all of their legs too. Then he headed off in Dan's direction. He could hear a yelp followed by silence from that direction and hastened his speed to answer his burning curiosity.

Dan was in position as he saw Boris move through the gate. As the Pricolici started herding the soldiers with gunshots he swore. The big Russian bastard was going to take all the fun for himself. Then he heard the crack of bullets from behind him and cussed in chagrin. Boris had reminded him about the perimeter guards and like a boot he'd lost his situational awareness and focused on what the other guy was doing.

He turned around, looking for cover from the direction of the guards' advance and cursed. For whatever reason, they were avoiding Boris to link up on this side. He had guards coming in, spread in a 270-degree arc with no cover to compensate for his exposure. They were enveloping his position now he had been spotted. They poured it on, putting him under continuous fire.

Thinking quickly, he drew his knife and charged the center of the arc. If he took them out and found cover beyond their line, he'd be in a better position. Firing from the hip as he went, he took out four of the guards quickly, shocked at the ease with which he accomplished the body count. He'd never been that accurate firing from the hip on the run before. Also, it was as if the MP5 just didn't have recoil.

It struck him like a pie in the face. Of course! He'd trained with the rest of the troops since he'd been enhanced but that had been all on the mats. Only unarmed or knife fighting and team tactics. The gun work he'd done since he'd been upgraded were with railguns, not these 9mm lighter pieces. With his improvements, it was a point and shoot situation. He didn't notice the recoil because, with his increased strength, there wasn't enough torque to even be an annoyance.

Running past the corpses of recent kills, he spotted a tree with a rock next to it. Sliding behind the stone, he started picking off the guards moving to flank him with the MP5. They quickly took cover, none of them revealing their heads long enough for him to draw a bead on them. Smart fighters.

Dan took a deep breath, looked around, and assessed his situation. There were more perimeter guards than they had expected. They had already killed five. There were at least eleven more out there firing in his direction.

While they had pinpointed him, their fire was inaccurate and suppressive. They were either hoping he would make a mistake, or they would get a lucky hit. They were not advancing to take him out but rather trying to flank him. That might be their best tactic in the circumstance considering the lack of adequate cover, but it also showed a lack of confidence. They should be leapfrogging, half of the force suppressing him, the other half moving forward. He stopped critiquing like he was the boss and started developing plans.

He wasn't an average human anymore. It had taken him longer to accept that than John Grimes and the team, probably because of his age. He could take a couple of bullets to his body armor and just keep going. If they flanked him or used grenades, he was in trouble, though. But he could probably move faster than they were used to. It would take time for them to adjust their aim to compensate, especially when leading their target.

Waiting here was getting him nowhere fast, so he chose

to take the initiative. Moving to run in an arc towards the first group he threw one of the knives Boris had given him as a distraction in the other direction. It's glint attracted a lot of fire as he took off running. It had felt like a minute before the sound of a bullet whizzed by near him.

At that point, he was nearing the flank of the seven-man group. Charging, he drew his knife with his off hand, firing bursts from the MP5 to keep them more worried about being hit than focused on shooting at him. Three went down in those bursts of his shots. That left four that were an immediate threat. His gun clicked empty, so he dropped it to hang on its sling and switched the knife to his right hand.

It was then that he spotted that his opponents had attached bayonets to their guns. He hadn't taken into account that they may be reacting slower than he expected of trained military, forgetting the fact that they weren't professionals. They had acted instinctively in the right way, though. This was fast becoming a cluster-fuck experiment, he thought. Drawing the silenced Glock with his left hand, he shot one of the attackers in the head as he pulled the gun and then the guards were on top of him.

He parried the first thrust with the Bowie knife, reversed his grip and drove it into the man's throat on the backswing. He cursed as it hit bone and stuck briefly. He blocked the second fighter with the Glock, the bayonet of his opponent skidding along the slide. Twisting aside from the third one, that man's blade still managed to plunge into his leg. With the rush of pain, he felt something electrify the senses throughout his body.

Dan could feel a type of energy envelope and thread

through his body. Whether it came from inside or outside, he couldn't determine in the rush of combat. He had spoken with Bethany Anne and Gabrielle enough to guess that this was Etheric energy working in his system.

He dropped both pistol and knife. With one hand he reached out and snapped the first man's neck. Then he wrenched the bayonet out of his leg and jerked the man holding the rifle forward. He smashed his fist into the man's nose driving bone into his brain with a crunch, killing him instantly.

He ducked behind cover and grabbed out one of the syringes that Bethany Anne had insisted he bring. It had her blood with extra nanites. He injected it next to the wound. As he crouched down reloading the MP5, he could see the injury slowly mend itself, leaving only the slick blood behind on the surface.

That left four out there to neutralize. He felt simultaneously sickened and energized by what he had just done. As he poked his head from cover, rifle fire resumed from his opponents. Bending to pick up his knife and pistol, he turned and charged the remaining guards. En-route he saw a wolf from the corner of his eye.

The firing had stopped as they paused to reload. He grinned. They should have sequenced their fire better. That way one of them could have kept shooting while the others reloaded.

He backhanded the wolf as it neared him and kept running at the men. As he came closer, he fired off two rounds taking out a man with each of his remaining shots and dropped the empty pistol. Turning slightly, he stabbed one man through the sternum with the knife. Finally, he grabbed the last man with his left hand and snapped his neck. He heard the final wolf approaching from behind, so he spun and slapped it violently across the face, forcing a yelp of pain as it tumbled away.

He retrieved his weapons. After reloading, he put the guns away and grabbed the unconscious, but breathing, wolf and throwing it over his shoulder. Dan walked back to where he assumed Boris was after he saw one of the tipped trucks being righted.

As Dan and Boris drove off with a truck full of wolves (and one still unconscious human), Dan asked, "So what do you plan on doing with them?"

"Interrogating them for information," Boris replied. "They have to know something useful. Organization, recruitment methods, base locations, supply routes. Something."

Dan grunted and responded, "I'm gonna call down a couple of extra pods. We'll dose them with a sedative and take them with us. Looks like you get to see the Australian base, mate." He said the last with a grin.

"I need to get back to…" Boris's voice trailed off. He wanted to be near Janna. He should get back to Danislav. There was a conflict in his priorities, confusion in his mind, that he worked to keep hidden from Dan as the truck proceeded down the dirt road to where they had landed a pod.

"You need this info, right? And you need to know they are telling the truth, yes? Then you need Stephen, Akio, Barnabas, or Bethany Anne. They can make sure you get straight dice out of these sorry sacks of shit."

Boris slowly nodded. Dan was right. It was best that they go about it this way.

CHAPTER SIX

QBS ArchAngel

Bethany Anne was going over reports with Barnabas when ADAM interrupted them.

<< Bethany Anne I regret to inform you TOM and I may have made an inexcusable error>>

What do you mean?

Uh, what my overly analytical accomplice is trying to say is we didn't thoroughly analyze all the programming in the Boris nanites, and therefore we might have misidentified them.

Guys, okay why are you coming to me with this now. I mean you've had them for weeks, right?

<<With everything that has been happening, I put confirming our initial analysis to the lowest priority.>>

Get with Jeffery and arrange for more E.I. units to assist you.

Not everything is on ADAM. I failed to give him details of older esoteric methods that were used by other Kurtherian Clans. The techniques were considered antique, not just obsolete. They dated from thousands of years before the split. They are so old that what I knew of them was incomplete.

So you are telling me we now have three possible landings of Kutherians on Earth for me to deal with? Well doesn't that make us special fucking snowflakes? She paused a second, thinking. *Ok, your priorities haven't changed. So, what upped the relevance and caused you two to figure out what the problem is, and brought it to my attention?*

TOM continued, **Unfortunately, that isn't the worst of it. There are programming quirks unique to each of the clans. Things that don't change, because they are embedded in how we learn to program. This coding is so old I cannot identify it as belonging to any clan. Or from an unknown faction within the clans. But that doesn't match up with the nanites. They are close to what I would call modern. It is like someone from your history - a Ghengis Khan, say - came to the present day and took nuclear technology back with him. Then he figured out how to modify them. Kurtherians of that era had not yet broken from the philosophy that the Five still have. I cannot predict what may have happened to change that.**

TOM stopped for a moment before realizing he hadn't answered her, But, to answer your question, it is Janna's condition that made us bring this to your attention.

<<The differences in programming are critical to what happened to Janna after she absorbed nanites from Boris by swallowing them. We gave the analysis much higher priority after the situation involving her was revealed.>>

They are much more aggressive at changing a person to fit their optimum DNA. Not only that, the medical pod cannot flush them from her system without a significant risk. A small but significant percentage of the nanites hook into the body's vital functions - literally - and siphon energy to reproduce. If she had been brought to me within hours, the Pod Doc still might not have had the capacity to halt or reverse the changes. The process would damage many cells in critical areas because one of the core rules was changed. The nanites will try to change a person whether they have enough energy, or not.

So whoever designed them was what? A psychopath?

No, that disorder was wiped out from our genome before we discovered interstellar travel.

<<Concerning the Kurtherian records available I must rate the probability as below .001%. There is always the chance, however small, of a random mutation replicating that effect.>>

TOM hesitated before he replied. You think we didn't check for such and repair them when we found them?

<<All I am saying is without further data we can only reach three conclusions. One, there was a Kurtherian of an older Era on this planet. Two, he modified the nanites of the group that changed the Wechselbalg for his own, unknown, purposes. Three, as a consequence of Janna's actions in saving Boris we may need to take measures to enable her to survive and leave the stasis we have her in.>>

We'll top off her etheric energy in the Pod, but we need to get her out of the pod for some time.

Well, why do you need to talk to me?

There was resounding silence for a moment.

Oh, right. You need my hands. And Janna needs to get some food in her. How long to go?

An hour or so would be my best guess before she can be removed. Her transformation, as I said, was very aggressive. She will need food and time before I feel safe putting her back in to make sure no permanent damage was done and re-key her nanites to her new DNA. ADAM and I will spend some of that time making sure there are no more hidden protocols in their programming. We will want to put Boris in to ameliorate the aggressiveness on his nanites after we fix the programming.

CHAPTER SEVEN

Mess Hall, TQB Base, Australia

Dan had gone off to report to the base guards and make sure that their prisoners were secure. Boris was hungry.

He always was after being shot.

Dan gave him directions to the mess area on the upper levels, so Boris found the room and served himself a large tray to start. There were some sidelong glances from the Were Guardians in the area at the large serving of vegetables.

None of them commented, however. Boris neither knew nor cared if it was due to comments about his sparring, or his allegiance to Bethany Anne. Right now, with his hunger, he was just happy to have the food without any smirks to irritate him from the group with their protein heavy eating habits.

There was no-one he knew in the mess. He sat down and started eating, enjoying the food. It was better than he had expected from a mass production-style setting like this.

The Stroganoff was excellent, although it could have done with some smoked paprika for his taste. Most of the conversation that he could overhear was centered around the recent unpleasantness in China. Boris had nothing to add, so he sat by himself at a table in the corner.

After about ten minutes Dan walked in with a small computer with speakers. He placed it on the table and went to get a tray of food for himself. When he sat down, he said "We need to talk, Boris. Janna is fine but what happened to her was unexpected and unpleasant. How many times have you tried to heal or change someone with your blood before?"

Boris blinked, confusion clear on his face, stress in his voice. His accent thickened as he said. "Vat do you mean? I have neever tried to change anyvone. My mother taught me that unlike other Veres, ve had to be born. And no-one ever told me that Veres could change another by blood. I assumed it vas by bite, vampires by blood, like de myths, da?"

Then a look of guilt formed on his face and his voice became filled with pain and guilt-ridden. "Do you mean dat vhat she did to save me, the blood she vas covered in, nearly killed her?"

Dan winced. If he had realized that Boris didn't know these things he would have approached the entire topic differently. Cursing himself, he put a hand on Boris's shoulder. "Look, Boris. If you didn't know. It. Was. Not. Your. Fault. You couldn't have even warned her. But TOM needs to explain the details to you."

Dan's explanation didn't seem to help Boris. He sat in a miserable crouch, the food he had been enjoying was now ashes in his mouth. When he talked about his past love, he looked like someone was poking a bruise.

Now he had the posture of someone with a dull spoon sawing through his guts.

TOM's voice came through the speaker. "I am far more at fault than you are Boris. ADAM and I did a quick and dirty analysis of the nanites in your blood when we put you in the medipod for the first time. We missed critical details in the differences in both the nature and programming of your nanites that would have become evident in a more detailed analysis. We assigned that project a low priority until Janna came into our care. We missed many details, like how aggressively your nanites would hook into and transform a new host."

"However, even if you had the standard Wechselbalg nanites, it has become evident to me that not all Weres understand the danger of trying to change someone. Unlike with vampires, an unsuccessful termination does not create an unintelligent walking appetite." TOM's voice took on clear discomfort talking about the unintended consequences of his transformation of Michael. "However, they will kill the new host if they are not genetically compatible with their programming."

By this point, the room had gone quiet as the dining Weres listened to this revelation. They knew that many didn't survive an attempted change, but the 'why' was new to them. Tom continued, "As those nanites were not initially keyed as precisely as Michael's, they have a wider tolerance, but a significant majority of the population cannot tolerate them. All Weres need to be careful - or very desperate - when they try and change someone."

Unnoticed to Boris, Bethany Anne and Janna had entered the room. Boris turned when Janna laid a gentle hand on his cheek.

Janna spoke softly from behind him, "Boris, it is not your fault. Besides, the operation in Russia needs you. I would gladly have died to save you if that is the price for taking out the NVG root and branch. I did not pay that price. Do not have guilt for might have been. It is a waste of time and effort." His guilt lessened at her words. Then he noticed the looks of concern on many of the faces in the mess. He turned and viewed her, and all his guilt returned.

The only people he had seen that were definitively in worse shape than she had been those who had barely survived the concentration camps and gulags of World War Two.

"*Moya prekrasnaya odna*, what have I done..." He whispered so softly that most likely only Janna and Bethany Anne heard.

She put a finger against his mouth, smelling him with her enhanced senses for the first time. He smelled wonderful. A mix of forests and damp earth filled her senses. "Not your fault. It is no-one's fault, Boris. It is over. I survived. I will be better soon." She tilted her head and gave him a slight smile "Although I am famished."

TOM interjected from the computer speakers, "I would like to have you in the medipod after Janna has been put through the second round in the medipod to finish fixing her nanites programming. We can modify the programming in your nanites to make them less dangerous. They are overly aggressive in how they change a new host. We can make them less so."

Janna turned to move toward the food line. Boris stood and touched her wrist. She turned and looked at him quizzically. With a gesture, he indicated she was to sit. Anger flashed in her eyes, but Bethany Anne shook her head minutely from behind Boris.

Janna nodded and sat down in the chair next to where Boris had been seated. Boris walked to the food line to get her a tray as piled with food as his had been. Bethany Anne looked at her and said. "Let him care for you. It will ease his guilt." With a wry smile, she said, "If he hadn't offered, I would have been tempted to slap him into next week."

Janna looked at her curiously. "Are you not worried about inappropriate fraternization amongst your followers?"

Bethany Anne answered, with a stern expression on her face, "Yes, I am. There isn't enough of it happening!" Janna's shock showed clearly, and Bethany Anne's expression relaxed.

"Have fun. TOM will tell me when you are finished. I'll come back to take you to the Pod Doc. I have no possible objections to anything in that direction that could happen between you and Boris. If they seem to be heading the other way, give me some warning." A small smile graced her face as she waved and headed out the mess door.

Dan made his excuses to Janna and left her to face Boris alone, in a room full of strangers, and with no place to hide.

Boris walked back to the table with the tray and carefully slid it in front of her. He put a cup of water next to it. Meanwhile, she was thinking about what Bethany Anne had said.

She had been efficiently told that whatever happened with Boris, as long as it didn't upset what needed to happen, was allowed. It was a paradigm shift for someone who had faced rigid military rules from the age of sixteen.

Janna had faked her age to sign up after passing the aptitude tests. She still struggled to admit that she was twenty-five, not twenty-seven at times. Even though the initial success of that deception had gained her admittance to both officer and intelligence training.

She wondered how young, how immature she must seem to Boris. Bethany Anne had only told her that he was over four hundred years old. Then she had casually, but painfully, admitted that her love had been over a thousand, while she was in her thirties.

Once Janna had taken a few bites, she paused to find Boris staring at her. "What is it?"

"Your hair, Janna. It has taken on a hint of red. I was just admiring the color," he replied calmly. The calm was fractured by a sudden and bright blush, kicking off an eruption of embarrassed laughter from him. The sound of his amusement boomed through the mess hall causing many to turn and stare.

"You actually must be recovering. You blush easily," he said with what she thought was a twinkle in his eye.

Janna returned that look with a challenging expression. "Since we have some luxury of time at this moment, how about we share stories of our pasts, Old Bear."

"As you wish, Cub. What do you want to know?" She winced slightly, not wishing him to think of her as a child.

"How old are you?" she soldiered on through her concerns.

Boris stroked his beard, thoughtfully. "I honestly am not sure. The earliest date I definitely know is the year I challenged Michael. That makes me more than four hundred. Before he exiled me to Siberia, I had jobs, service in the Cossack hosts and other places, but no real interest in the year. I wanted to be doing things, active things. I didn't even learn to read until my exile because it was for the sedentary. Now, of course, I am literate in at least eight languages. My turn. What was your life like before you joined the army?"

Her eyes went hooded as if some dark memory clouded them. "I do not talk of my life with family. They abandoned me to the streets when I was eight. I saw much suffering, but was a great reader, even back then, and the librarians took care of me when they were able. I was always in the library, learning, safe, and warm. I suspect that they felt pity for me. It was not until I applied to join the army that I sat for my first test. I have a great memory, so I found it easy. My turn. How many wars have you been in?"

It was time for Boris's face to darken. "Too many. So many of the wars, when I was younger, had no real purpose. Sometimes to the aggrandizement of one man or another. Others were squabbles over who controlled this section or that of land. Perhaps over who's invisible friend was real. There were few wars I fought in, looking back, that truly had a justification. The Great Patriotic War. Driving Napoleon back. Fighting the Reds and the Blacks. They were all good wars and battles. Fighting for a cause worth all the loss, even if we failed. The rest..." he just shook his head in sorrow. "How did you end up in intelligence?"

"When I enlisted I had lied about my age. I made it through all the training, wanting to serve as a soldier. It was a better life than on the streets. Then I was assigned to a unit that my uncle commanded. He was suspicious that we might be related and ordered a private DNA test, not wanting to compromise either his group or his career. This showed that we were close relatives, and he knew of only one missing female relative within five years of my claimed age. He was aware that my age was younger than I had told them."

She shrugged, remembering the time, "He reported it, and the GRU gave me a choice. Take officer training and transfer to where I obviously had skills or be court marshaled and end up destitute. I had lived destitute before, I told them. Growing up on the streets, learning what I could from the library. That floored them. My test results were extraordinary. My uncle confirmed that I had been missing from the age of eight as did many records. At that point, they stopped using threats to make me join. I had skills that could aid the country better than as a common soldier, they said. I eventually accepted."

"Let this be enough questions for now, Janna. Come now, you must eat." Smiling inside, Janna dutifully obeyed. After all, she was famished.

And she had finally started to learn more about his past.

CHAPTER EIGHT

Command Container, Russia

Janna had gone from her previous condition to still slightly underweight, but far healthier in the last three days. The most significant improvement had come from her time in the pod after she had eaten three heaped trays of food. Boris had continued to regale her with stories from his past while she ate.

His stories only increased her respect for him.

After Janna's time in the pod was done, Boris had been put in to reduce the risk to others from his blood. While he was in the medipod, John ran her through a testing regimen, to make sure that she was fit, despite TOM and ADAM's assurances. Most of that had been simple sparring, but at the end of the session, he finally convinced her to spar as hard as she was capable. John was pleased to confirm her strength was back.

Janna still wasn't convinced she had been changed since there was no difference in the way she felt. Perhaps her emotions tilted towards annoyance and frustration more quickly, but that could be because she was not used to inactivity. She realized she did not feel any weaker than before the incident, but also didn't feel like an animal or anything unusual. No longer looking like a starveling, there did not seem any reason that she should be prevented from at least participating in the ambushes with the rest of her team.

"Why can't I come with you on this assault? TOM, ADAM, and John all declared me fit. I mean John took me out in training, but he does that to everyone except Gabrielle and Bethany Anne." Janna was furious. It seemed that her hair color wasn't all that had changed. Her temper had as well. Rather than the pale platinum blonde, she had been born with her hair was now a rich strawberry blonde.

"And would you say this outburst is like you?" Boris asked. "According to your file, which ADAM forwarded to me, you were one of the calmest, most level-headed, most calculating soldiers or junior officers any of your COs had ever had. Weres are more aggressive than humans. Until you get used to it and learn to harness it, you are no good on the battlefield. Consider it a form of rehabilitation. You don't send a soldier straight back out after recovery."

Janna's irritation was evident in her voice, "Then why haven't you been training me! It's been three days since I got back. More than one and a half since you finished interrogating those scum."

All the Weres had been criminals who had joined the NVG after Konrad had arranged for their release from prison. Although Boris was somewhat ambivalent about the executions of two of them, he was pleased overall. Those two had been petty crooks before joining Konrad.

The human captive was still in their custody for now. Boris honestly did not care if the prisoner lived or died, but there was more information in his head to be extracted, so his usefulness had not come to an end. Frank, Akio, and Dan were taking care of the extraction of information so that Boris could keep his attention elsewhere.

Barnabas had judged them all. The stay of execution for the remaining prisoner was temporary.

Danislav cautiously interrupted. "And when has he had time, young Bear? When have I had time? When have you had time? I had to reorganize the group I was supposed to lead because of all this. It has been decided that someone needs to stay with the command center for the first few ops. We have all been organizing the plan for the disruption of the three convoys. We have a twelve-hour window for all three operations. Paul is the only one who has slept. He is also the only normal human. He even offered to stay with you."

Janna's eyes flashed, and she let off a string of insults in mixed Russian, English, French, and German. Paul corrected her German, which was not particularly helpful but amused him and infuriated her. At one point it looked like Boris would have to step in. Danislav was convinced that Paul was completely insane at this point. He wouldn't have risked correcting her.

Boris hid his grin when it happened. They had been serving together for a long time.

"I will start training you tomorrow Janna. If we have prisoners, I will let Danislav and Paul interrogate them. We even have permission from Barnabas to execute future prisoners. They aren't soldiers. They are an illegal military force that has committed crimes against humanity. Walking down a street and just killing people. Being willing to wipe out an entire town." Boris said, the anger boiling in his tone.

"We need to get going to the first rendezvous. We will be back." Boris's nose was not as sensitive as Danislav's so he could not understand the underlying fear beneath her frustration. She was afraid Boris was not going to come back. Danislav turned slightly away from Boris and signaled to her that he would keep an eye on Boris.

He hadn't seen the old bear this happy in years. He didn't want it to fuck up on him now.

***

"One weapons convoy. It was supposed to be vital supplies headed for a base near China. Hmm. I guess that close to the border, weapons could be considered as such." Paul spoke into the air.

Boris and the others had returned with one captive from the three raids. Apparently, everyone had been a bit over-enthusiastic. But now three of the six groups had a distribution of silver ammo, just in case. Some of the wolves had been unhappy about it, but common sense had, in the end, overcome their hesitation. Only a small fraction of the groups consisted of Weres after all.

The captured heavy weapons had been carried to their vehicles and were being hidden at various locations in the different areas of operations. Some of the supplies and most of the ammunition had been taken, while the rest had been burned.

As a further strategy, they were using the same camouflage Chechen rebels used and were careful to leave a torn piece of cloth near each raid. Those bastards had been more active lately, and the deception seemed to be working. Investigators had concluded that Chechens were attacking 'road convoys' and the pressure on the government to do something about it was rising from the public and the military. Reserve units had been called up, and that would restrict the NVG as much or more than Boris and his group. All of Boris' forces came from Siberia, a region with a reputation for staunch Christianity. None were suspected of being Islamists.

After they had debriefed with Frank and ADAM, they had breakfast. Paul begged off the interrogation, wanting to sleep, but Danislav was more than happy to do it. So Janna insisted on Boris starting her training.

Boris spoke, "The first thing you need to learn now is, even in your human form, you will be stronger." He pulled out one of the captured weapons he had returned from the raid with. Grabbing the barrel with one hand, he casually bent it. "You will need to be lighter on the trigger of any gun, or you will damage it. They are designed for humans, except my custom AA-12."

"That's one thing I am confused by. I have been trying to figure out how a bear could fire a shotgun for the last couple of days. It has been driving me nuts, to be honest. I can't see a way."

"No, in bear form I cannot use it. I have an... in-between shape. I can use it while in that form, but only with drum magazines and only that weapon."

"Will you show me how to change to that shape?"

Boris raised his hand, quieting her questions. "I cannot show you. I only found the first path to that form when my mother was raped and killed by bandits. It is not something that can be taught. It is something I would not wish on my best friend or worst enemy. It is dangerous, see? In a thousand years, I am the only Were that has been able to take the form and not succumb to the consequences. The anger and frustration you feel? That is nothing compared to what you feel in that shape. It is also addictive." He closed his eyes. "The power you feel, it is indescribable." He paused, taking deep breaths. He needed to stay away from such thoughts for now. He needed to avoid that form for a time.

After the pause, he continued. "There are other ways, maybe. But I have no idea how to teach them to you at this time. I would not be willing to take that shape for some time. I have used it perhaps too often recently."

"You are just trying to hold me back!" she yelled at him. He had, however, prepared for this. He did, after all, know a female Pricolici.

He responded. "Ecaterina will be happy to talk to you about it if you wish. She gave me her contact details if you do not have them already. You can speak to her after we train." He continued "Your life was turned upside down before you were changed. You need to move past the anger you feel at that. The frustration of the situation you find yourself in. You also need to learn to fight like a bear."

He raised an eyebrow and turned, starting to remove his clothes, continuing to talk. "Remember three main things. First, unlike an ordinary bear, for whatever reason, I have never found it hard to balance on my hind paws. Use that. It is an advantage. You have claws, use them. You can bite hard, it is a potent weapon, but doing so can expose yourself. Be observant of your situation before you use it."

He shifted into his bear form. This was one of the few times he'd shifted around another werebear. He had done it before, but it was like there was static in his head. It was perhaps a side effect of the changes that had gotten rid of the headaches, he supposed.

He turned and looked at Janna. She looked a bit freaked out. Shifting from foot to foot she asked "How do you do that? How do you shift like that?" Boris rolled his eyes lifted a paw and pointed it in the direction of the bunker. To be honest, he didn't remember how. He'd been doing it for so long he just did it. He ambled down to the container and rapped his claws on the open the door to get Danislav's attention. Janna followed him closely.

Danislav looked pissed when he answered but saw that Janna was looking confused, and Boris had chosen to remain a bear. He had some idea of why. Boris had been born and raised a Were - he just changed, he didn't think about it. Danislav may have been born a Were, but it had taken him years to figure out how to turn, to the frustration of both himself and Boris.

"Watch this guy while I'm gone. If he moves, eat him." He said to Boris, as much as for the intimidation effect as anything else. Boris was by far the most massive bear anyone had seen, easily more than eight hundred kilograms, about twenty percent bigger than the maximum Siberian bears were considered to reach. The only natural bears that might close in on his size were the largest Californian grizzlies or the occasional Kodiak.

He walked off a short distance and said "I can guess the problem. You don't know how to change, right?" Janna nodded mutely. "One of the things Boris doesn't understand is the mechanics of it. Once I figured out how to transform I tried explaining it to him, but he's done it for so long that he can just do it when he wants. For him, it is all instinctual. He knew I was a Were when he adopted me from the orphanage decades ago. Probably born that way. When I was a teenager, and he was trying to teach me to change, he was stumped too. It has been centuries since he first did it and the first time is always the hardest. Oh, and before you start sparring with him, go for a run."

He rubbed his ribs "It won't take you long, but your first half hour or so you'll be clumsy as hell. So don't try to spar with him then. You will get hurt if you do, and he'll blame himself. Neither of you would be to blame of course, but he still will blame himself."

"He raised you? Why would he do that? I mean I can understand him getting a lone Werewolf child away from ordinary kids, but why didn't he just hand you over to the pack?" Janna asked

"I'm not sure he knows himself. He's not like most other werebears, though. Traveling with him I've met a few, and they tend to be loners, through and through. Some wolves are that way too. While he might appreciate a few days, even a week alone, there is not a driving need for constant solitude within him. After that he gets lonely. Being pack leader and as feared as he was after the Great Patriotic War, perhaps he just wanted some reliable company."

Danislav continued "If you like what you are wearing I

would suggest that you get undressed. If you stay in those clothes, they'll be wrecked when you change. Oh, and after you change, a lot of animals will be skittish around you. The predator scent lingers for a time. I don't know of a Were that doesn't like changing every so often for the hell of it. I'm sure there are some, but it is a lot of fun being an animal."

He looked to the sky and then back down, "The key is to really want to change. Once you manage to transform there is a kinda switch in your mind's eye that you can just flick. Then you change. No mystical clap-trap. It's that simple."

He turned and headed back to the container. He did not need to see a beautiful woman that his father desired naked. No sirree. At best he'd be seeing a potential step-mother naked. Ick. At worst he'd start falling for her. He didn't want to cause that sort of tension between Boris and him. He respected the man who had raised him too much to risk it.

Janna stood there for a couple of minutes considering everything that Danislav had just told her. She was plunging into a world of which she had only seen the edges. Well, she had friends in that world already. People who cared for her. First, there was Boris. He had been treating her differently, as if she was emerging from the shadow of his past to a real person in the here and now. And there was Danislav who was treating her as if she belonged and that there was truly a place for her in their world as well. A group that wanted her for her. Not for the skills and tricks she had picked up and learned over the years. Her. It was as if for the first time in her life she understood what family meant. Even if it was a strange conglomerate of a family.

She truly wanted to belong. To do that she had to figure this out. She slowly started undressing, focusing on that desire. She heard Boris lumbering up behind her. Quietly she said. "If I figure this out, please let me try and enjoy the form for a bit first." She didn't turn, didn't look at him, but she heard him lie down. After she had finished undressing, she closed her eyes.

She didn't notice when Boris rose and moved around to get a better view of her body. It was spectacular. He estimated she had gained an inch or so. With her still in recovery, it was hard to tell what she'd look like an end result. She was healthy now, though. Still underweight, but not looking like a walking skeleton with a thin layer of skin and muscle over the bones. Seeing that she was improving gave Boris a level of calm he hadn't achieved in a week.

Her focus tightened, and she found the switch that Danislav had talked about. With trepidation, she flicked it... and nothing happened. She cursed out loud, but all that came out was a bear's roar.

She opened her eye and saw she was standing as a bear. Standing felt uncomfortable, so she lowered herself to all fours, both stunned and exhilarated by the transformation. She was extraordinarily large for a female bear, taller than normal and at least seven hundred and fifty kilograms in weight. She had brown-grey fur and was similar to Boris in body shape and markings. If she were thought to be a normal bear, a zoologist would describe her as belonging to the Siberian subspecies of brown bear. Though smaller than Boris, the difference in size was not as large as in nature – instead, it was closer to the difference in size in their human forms. Her form would still need to finish filling out, but that would come in time. Her muscles would strengthen, and she might even gain a bit more weight.

The world had more scents and... her train of thought was interrupted as she failed to coordinate the movement of all four legs. Her back paws tangled each other, propelling her into a hard fall onto her face. In the back of her mind, she thought she could hear a chuckle. She turned in irritation and stared at Boris, who was facing away from her. Huffing at his back, she started to climb carefully back onto her feet when he turned to look over his shoulder at her. With a challenging roar, he began to run.

Concentration and precise movement were abandoned in her response to the challenge. Scrambling without thought to her feet, she wrenched her body back up and into the exhilaration of the chase. His scent showed the path he traveled, and as she gained confidence, she picked up the pace. Within an hour she was fully confident in the form but was still trailing Boris. His path had formed an arc around their camp, but he was always well ahead of her. The air had a faint metallic scent on it as she got closer to him. When she found him in the clearing, she saw that he had run down a deer. With surprising dexterity, he had also gutted it and put the stomach and intestines in one pile with the offal dumped separately.

He stood his ground, rose to his full immense height, and roared a challenge at her. She knew that he wanted to spar with her. The scent of blood and fresh meat excited her, and she tried to get past him to the prize displayed on the ground. His plan on how to train her was apparently well thought out. He knew the nature of Weres from hundreds of years of study, Janna doubted he was challenged with how to engage her bear form.

For the next hour, she tried to get past him as her hunger and frustration increased. His defense of the carcass and her desire for the food pushed her into trying to maul him with her claws, attacking him from either side to no avail. Eventually, she saw him come in a little slowly with one of his forepaws, and she swung back out of its path and bit it. Hard. He backed off and let her pass.

After the intensive exercise, she was famished, and her nose led her straight to the pile of offal. Without thinking about it, she ate the entire pile, finding it far tastier than she had as a human. Finishing, she saw that Boris had slung the gutted carcass over his back. As her head rose from her meal, he made a soft sound to get her attention and started heading back towards the camp.

CHAPTER NINE

NVG Base Omega, Russia

Shen was nervous. His captor had been pacing and ranting around his cell for days. Finally, after nearly a week of the ranting, the vampire called him over and started demanding answers from him.

"You are from China originally, right? Your clan borders the lands claimed by this, this Werebear that claims Siberia. What do you know of him? What resources does he have?"

Shen stood for a minute, shocked by two things. Why was the vampire asking him something, rather than using him as a living experimental blood supply? Amazing, and odd. Then there was the question. There were legends as to why the clans had never moved into Siberia. The myths and stories told about the Siberian Bear were genuinely terrifying. Most agreed he was truly ruthless against any Asiatic Weres.

With cause, Shen had to admit.

The last major incursion by the clans had been more

than three centuries ago and had been a disaster. The stories were often told to children as a warning against having contempt for a foe. Those who had attacked had gone, sure of victory, but not one in ten of the Werewolves involved had returned alive. Even fewer of the Werecats had returned.

Even the vampires of the East had been cautious about sending people into Siberia. It was as if the area was a black hole for Asian members of the UnknownWorld. He suspected it was part of the reason why there was so little transfer between the Asiatic UnknownWorld and the rest. His personal experiences were somewhat different, but that might be because he was merely traveling as a businessman, not acting as any threat.

At his hesitation and the glaze-eyed look on his face, the vampire cursed and left the room. He came back quickly with plenty of smoked meat, which he passed through the bars. Shen broke out of his reverie at the smell and started to wolf down the food. He had been hungry for so long that the food was all he could focus on.

After he had finished eating, he looked out of the bars at the vampire who repeated his questions to Shen again, this time with forced calm in his voice.

Shen considered his answer carefully. He was in this vampire's power, and he didn't want to piss him off.

"Just answer with the truth, Were. I have no reason to punish you. Anything less puts my plans at risk. Answer honestly and I will provide more food for you."

Shen nodded his understanding, if not his belief, "If it is the same one that my people encountered centuries ago, then I have to say that this Werebear is dangerous. He managed to turn back several attempted incursions by the clan over the last three centuries with massive losses on our side. Only one of the Weres sent to take and hold the territory returned. He was insane, kept mumbling that a bear attacked his forces, taking them apart a piece at a time. That the bear could not be touched. He was missing an arm when he returned to us. His mind never recovered."

"Even vampires attempting to claim dominion over Asia were cautious about provoking him."

"He became known as the Ghost Bear. Some people doubt that the original one is still alive, but the fear he has caused over the years is such that people still are cautious when thinking of entering Siberia."

"Vampires from China became more and more cautious about their travels to Siberia. It is said that they behaved impeccably or ended up dead."

Konrad swore. The Ghost Bear was the pack leader in Siberia? The man had led a very successful campaign against the Weres and lesser vampires on the Eastern front. He had killed two of Konrad's brothers. He'd never been able to find out more than the code name. Peter had refused to tell David, stating that it was war, and people on both sides had died. Even though the Ghost Bear was only a Wechselbalg, Peter had offered to take it to Michael for arbitration. David had backed down. He did not want Michael involved on the off chance he might find out some of the formulae survived.

This whole project suddenly became personal, not just a power grab. Konrad wanted this Ghost Bear, Boris, dead. He would have to be careful, though. Boris's pack was reputed to be very loyal. The setback at Romanovka had him out of position and his troop strength lower than he truly liked. Konrad needed to come up with a plan.

His thoughts turned to the refugee column and the Border Forces Spetsnaz unit whose commander he had subverted. Yes, perhaps by distracting him he could still improve his position enough to succeed in his plan. Once that was done, he would be in a far better place to get revenge. With control over crucial areas, he could force the President to change Russian policies to what he wanted over time. And to send as many teams and assassins as it took to kill Boris.

Major Yerokhin had called together the five Captains of the teams that were available and could be spared from the reserve. He had four of his fifteen teams already acting on drug interdiction operations, one gathering intelligence. He needed to maintain a reserve of four teams. His contact with the NVG had managed to arrange orders from the Ministry of the Interior to mobilize his available forces to interdict and delay the column of civilians en-route to make an illegal border crossing.

He had been promised a promotion by his contact in addition to his usual payment if he managed to delay the convoy ten days. With his other responsibilities, he needed to be here in case his other units required the reserves. He'd be sending in five teams to operate independently. It gave them more flexibility and him more cover if the government decided to disavow the orders. He had career goals of his own that did not involve any sort of time in jail.

He started issuing movement orders. The troops would insert by helicopter tonight and commence operations immediately.

Captain Evgeni Dubrovsky was not comfortable with his orders. His team wouldn't be either. Taking down drug traffickers and thwarting slavers - that was why he had joined. Killing civilians fleeing something was not. If they were fleeing illegal paramilitary troops, as was the most common rumor, he liked it even less. Harming civilians, Russian civilians, put into an impossible situation was not what he'd signed up for. He'd run any man without similar feelings out of his team. A team needed to know they could rely on each other. He was aware that there were many corrupt people in the forces but made sure there were none amongst his team.

After they had landed, he was going to head straight for the refugee column and attempt contact. His men would follow him and his orders, or not. He would not have his honor stained with innocent blood if he could help it.

CHAPTER TEN

Refugee Column en route to Mongolia

The progress of the column had been slowed by the weather. With all the older people in the column, the trip was having to slow its pace. Many of them were succumbing to the cold and illnesses. This was despite the fresh meat that the Werewolves were able to bring in to supplement the supplies. The off-road capabilities of the military trucks and four-wheel drives were sorely tested.

The convoy commander, Lev, was worried. They were at least three days behind schedule, and if there were more slippage, they wouldn't make their pickup time. He needed to find a way to pick up the pace, and if the weather didn't clear up, he couldn't see how. He only hoped their rescuers would understand. He believed the Czarina would.

It was at that moment he heard a wolf howl in the distance. The cry repeated three more times. He swore and started organizing a group of the armed men. That was a signal for armed men moving to intercept. This was the last thing he needed.

Within the hour he had four groups of a hundred men heading in the direction of the howls. There was a reserve of two hundred and fifty men waiting for one of the wolves to give details of the number and bearing of the troops. They had to be Border Forces, not regular Army. There simply were no bases near enough to the route for the Army to have sent enough troops, even if they were willing. Spetsnaz to slow them down further was a worrying possibility. The wolf with the report would be here soon.

It was a Spetsnaz team, but they were acting very strangely. They were compromising stealth for speed, something special forces rarely did. And they were heading directly for the sides of the column when the most efficient way of sabotaging its progress would be to either raid the rear or set impediments to their progress at the front. He sent the wolf back to the group with orders for them to ambush but negotiate before firing. It was a risk, but if it got them more information, it would be worthwhile.

He only hoped it would end well. If they were defectors, he was sure that either the Czarina or Boris would be able to find a use for them.

Evgeni chose to take the lead position. It was only fitting. Since this was his idea, he would take the place of the highest risk. He was pushing his men hard, abandoning all stealth for speed. The five teams had been given different drop off points and were to act independently to 'maximize confusion in the refugee column.' Even if this was a legal and legitimate operation, that was one of the stupidest orders that could have been given. For less than eighty men to cause any significant effect on a column of this size, even of civilians, they needed either air support or coordination. They had none of the latter, and the weather in Siberia would become that of a Caribbean paradise before the former was provided. Not that he could blame any potential pilot. He wouldn't want his name on an attack on any group of refugees.

The howling of wolves had started within an hour of their drop off. It was somewhat unnerving. In the past when he'd been near wolves out in the wild they'd not been as active. He even saw one of the wolves howl four times a distance away on a small hill. It didn't matter. It wasn't like they were communicating his location or anything.

The team kept moving fast towards the refugees for about two hours more when he slowed down. There was something wrong, something he couldn't define. He stopped and gave the signal for the rest of his team to halt and take cover. Then he heard the distinctive sound of several rifles being taken off safety around him. He estimated he was still an hour's hard travel from the column at least. They were being ambushed this far out, and while Evgeni couldn't figure out the how.

He had a fair idea of the why.

He carefully raised his hands and kept them clear of any weapon. He couldn't see any way it was one of the other teams. They had been dropped too far away to reach this area and set up an ambush, and likely one of them would have shown himself by now. They all had the same shoulder flashes and knew each other.

"Whoever's out there I'd appreciate a parley," he said in a firm voice.

"Why would we negotiate with soldiers from the same government that arrested fifty of us without cause and shot another twenty-five out of hand?" a voice replied coldly from the bushes.

"Because the force that did that was illegal. We are legal border force troops of the Russian Federation. And we come bearing news of a danger to your justified fleeing of the country."

There was silence for over a minute. Then came the response out of the trees. "If that is the case, call the rest of your team forward and pile your weapons against the pine tree ten meters to your left. All of them, even your utility knives. Then all of you step back ten meters from the tree with your hands raised. We will take you to the man organizing the column. Hell, we'll even feed you if none of you give us any trouble. Anyone who does cause a problem will be killed on the spot."

Evgeni gave the order to his troops. He just hoped that none of them decided that this was all a bad idea.

***

It was an hour and a half later when Evgeni was finally brought to Lev. Lev was a steel-haired man with evident military experience. Probably one of the retired mercenaries from the town. There were supposedly about fifty of them from his briefing. Most of the Spetsnaz had shown contempt at the fact they were just mercenaries, but Evgeni was from the oblast. He knew some of the tales that were told about Boris and those he trained.

He also knew that Boris refused to teach the Spetsnaz as many were too arrogant to learn from an outsider once they had been selected. They believed they were the best of the best, that was part of the esprit de corps, the mystique about them, that allowed them to be so good. But it also meant they felt contempt for those without similar training. They believed there was nothing they could learn from outside the units.

Somehow this mercenary had figured out not only that his team was coming, but had managed to get a professional ambush laid against it before he should have known they were in the region. His scouts must be amazing. Evgeni would be happy to learn anything he could from them. Looking around, Evgeni didn't expect any classes on scouting today.

Lev was in the back of a truck with a paper map of the current area laid out on a table bolted to the bed, the map pinned to the table. He had three men who looked like they'd been out in the forest for days along with what looked to be his two top aides with him. Evgeni was pointedly put on the other side of the table. One of the aides had a pistol drawing a bead on his shoulder, finger off the trigger in case of a bump. It was clear what would happen to him should he behave aggressively here. Not that he planned to.

Lev got straight to the point. "What is the threat you wish to inform us of? Has the Border Force mobilized against us? Our sources have confirmed that they are the only force that could possibly intercept us now that the NVG's pursuit force is gone."

Evgeni was stunned. He had heard nothing of an additional force being sent after the column and only nebulous pieces about the NVG he had discarded as a rumor. He did not let it interrupt his briefing. "There are four other teams of Spetsnaz who, along with mine, were given orders to harass and delay your column. My team and I did not join the Border Force to kill Russian civilians. Criminals, yes. Citizens fleeing crimes against their people? No. I picked my men. Trained them. Any that did not meet my standard of personal integrity I wrote up and sent on their way." He spoke with some pride and straightened his back to look squarely at the column commander.

Over the next fifteen minutes, he gave detailed locations and proposed operations for each of the other four teams. He gave details on each of their commander's personalities. He included any knowledge of how they ran their teams and any exceptionally skilled individuals in those groups. At the end of his short briefing, the three who looked like scouts grunted and left the vehicle.

"You know I have to treat you and yours as 'guests' in our convoy for the rest of our trip? I cannot endanger the lives of my people by letting you go. You will be with us to the Mongolian border," Lev told the young Captain.

He nodded. "Yes. Indeed we were hoping to defect to whoever was taking you in. None of us wish to continue to serve a government so corrupt someone in it would send troops to kill civilians that have been abused by an armed political faction."

Lev looked him straight in the eye as he said. "Be that as it may. They may agree to this. But while you travel with me your men will be separated into pairs, with six of my own guarding each pair. So long as none of you try to cause us trouble, you will camp together at night, with guards surrounding you. Nor will you get your weapons returned until after the border. I will not risk more than ten thousand lives for little discomfort from sixteen. You will also hand over all radios. Do you understand?"

Evgeni only nodded. It was about what he expected. "Of course, sir. If you could let me explain it to my men?

Lev nodded, and the aide with the pistol jumped off the truck with him. They were soon joined by two more armed men from the convoy.

His team still had fifty armed men marching behind them. At least they hadn't done anything stupid. They were being treated far better than could have been expected, as effective prisoners of war. Maybe defecting hadn't been as dumb as he had sometimes thought. Perhaps whomever these refugees were going to would be worth serving.

Mikhail was glad he had been chosen to lead this pack. His kid cousin was one of those shot in cold blood. She had just been walking down the street to pick something up. Instead, she had gotten a bullet to the brain. After over a hundred years in Russia, he just could not face another period of troubled time. Besides he could do more good working for this Czarina, he was sure, than he could by staying. Even though what Boris was doing was necessary for the Czarina, Mikhail's heart would not have been in it.

He could truly devote himself to a leader like her. The word was that she had a tendency, a preference even, to lead from the front. That was another thing that Mikhail could respect.

So he made his choice and was one of the most senior among the Weres that were protecting the refugees. Hell, he had known most of the townspeople all his life. When Lev had asked him to be one of those who were to talk to a possible defector it had been more because he had a talent, though. It was not as reliable as some other methods, but it was far more subtle. He could usually smell when a person was lying. That officer had been nervous, even a little afraid, but he didn't give off the sour odor of deception. As long as the column encountered actual Spetsnaz out here, the information was valid.

The Spetsnaz drop points had seemed odd if the objective was only a simple delay. They were, however, perfect for a delay and cause casualties mission. That was what had sent Evgeni against those orders. He was one of the good officers, at least if his information was accurate. Seven packs of thirty had been sent out, and Mikhail's had just hit the jackpot.

He smelt the bastards moving no more than half a kilometer away. They smelled similar to the base odor of the officer to whom he had talked. It looked like it was time to make these attackers disappear.

With quiet whines and yips, he communicated that the rest of the pack, other than his second, was to pair off and take a target. He and his second would take the lead and the back of the group, respectively. The attack was to start with either the first sign of aggression towards them or his snarl as he went for the lead.

They crept up through the dripping foliage placing careful paws on the ground and staying low to the ground. Humans were not the only ones that could do a belly crawl, Mikhail thought, his tongue lolling out of his mouth briefly in humor at the thought. It was so much easier creeping up on someone as a wolf.

He found a position at seventy-five meters ahead of the enemy team. Settling into position and tensing his legs for the leap, he could feel his blood pounding as the excitement of the kill started to take hold. His target was not close enough yet. The Spetsnaz were moving cautiously and slowly in the misty rain. They knew that the refugees must be close. In truth, the column was only an hour or so behind where his pack now lay in ambush. If it were not for the rain, these men might be already setting up sniper nests to kill his friends and neighbors.

The Spetsnaz' luck had just run into the error known as *Things you cannot plan for.*

There was no way they could expect a pack of wolves (or werewolves) to deliberately ambush a group of sixteen humans. Mikhail had a very black and white view of things after a century. If they hadn't defected to the refugees, they were the enemy. He'd seen too many soldiers who didn't take their responsibility to protect civilians seriously enough. The fact that they were willing to delay or kill refugees was sufficient for him.

With a snarl that shredded the dreary mist, Mikhail jumped for the lead man's neck as he passed. The man turned impressively quickly, managing to get a burst of shooting off, but was too late to stop Mikhail's jaws closing on his jugular. At the same moment that hot blood sprayed into his mouth, Mikhail felt the burn of two bullets creasing his leg. It didn't matter as his mass toppled the dying man over to the ground. The wolf tore again at the man's throat, and the soldier died in a gurgling sigh.

Mikhail heard more snarls rip through the rainy night as the rest of the pack launched their attacks. Among the noises, mingled shouts of confusion could be heard along with an occasional burst of rifle fire. A few screams of agony, finally followed by silence.

Their part of this mission complete, the pack split and circled wide, scouting further ahead. If there were more Border Force troops out there, they needed to be found and neutralized, if possible. It was entirely plausible that their informant hadn't known, or hadn't told them everything. Best to make sure that there was not another little SNAFU ahead.

Evgeni and his men had a sleepless night, four times waking to bursts of gunfire. They had all known that there were men in those groups who might have also defected given a chance. They even knew that it was the cruel calculus of war. Had they misjudged one man outside of their team and approached them, the team would, at best, have been broken up. At worst they would have been scattered to different prisons. The refugee column could have taken heavy losses. Civilian losses, good Russian lives. Lives that they were sworn to protect by their solemn oath.

The bottom line balanced sixty-two lives against the thousands in the column. Trading so small a number against the potential death of many old people, women, and children was a bargain. Even if some of them dead were friends.

It was therefore of great surprise to them when a baker's dozen of their comrades were dragged into their encampment by some of the column's militia. Supplies to patch them up were provided. Some of their wounds were terrible. All of them were dog or wolf bites.

Evgeni thought it very strange, as he could remember seeing few if any dogs with the column. At least not dogs that could cause such wounds. Perhaps they were all out with the scouts. Yes, that made sense. The scouts were probably skilled hunters and hunters often had their own dogs.

He comforted himself with that as thoughts of humanity's darker legends whispered to him in the back of his mind.

CHAPTER ELEVEN

Command Container, Siberia, Russia

The attack on the column had complicated matters. Boris had decided to travel to confer with Lev, leaving Danislav, Janna, and Paul to co-ordinate operations. They had managed to identify several NVG bases of operations and had conducted spoiling raids to keep them on their toes. The captured heavy weapons were used here, to increase the evidence that it was Chechen irregulars that were responsible. It had left Janna with a problem, though since this interrupted her training with Boris. To adjust to the change, her training switched to a different form of battle. Like the wolves that Danislav convinced to help him with her training, men often attacked in numbers.

Training against wolves for a werebear her size wasn't challenging until the attackers numbered more than five. Then, especially with her inexperience, it became a white-wash for the wolves. They were experienced at working as a group, almost on an instinctive level. Her size became a disadvantage against that many. She couldn't move fast enough to avoid getting hamstrung. Against that many, she couldn't keep them from getting one of their team into position. From there on it was terrible news. She usually managed to take out three before one reached her throat, but that was just not good enough.

So she had contacted Ecaterina. They had talked for a while about many things, including her pregnancy, baby and how happy it made her. Eventually, Janna brought up the Pricolici form.

"I cannot shake the feeling that he is deliberately holding me back. I have encountered it before you know. Men who believe, somehow, that women need to be restricted in their responsibilities because they are *weaker.*"

Ecaterina snorted "I know exactly what you mean. My Nathan did the same sort of thing to me some time ago when I was human. I don't think it is the case this time. For two reasons. The first is that the most common trigger for that form is an extreme loss. Nathan thought I was dead before the first time he changed. From what you have told me, the death of Boris's mother caused his first change. He wants to spare you that pain. He loves you, even if he isn't showing it." She smirked as Janna blushed a furious red at the comment.

She continued in a more serious tone "He is also worried about whether or not you will succumb to the form. The Pricolici form is very intoxicating. I have felt it, the call to change into it because I can, not because I need to. And he has hunted down people who have lost themselves to it. That is another fear he has. You cannot blame him for that. It is similar to all of the older vampires I have met. They each have regrets and are, for lack of a better term, a little broken. They have an aspect of… having seen too much."

Janna nodded "And he is as old as some of the younger vampires in the group you are talking about. He has a lot of 'baggage,' I think that is the American idiom. I cannot believe I just called someone over four hundred years old *younger*. It all seems so unreal sometimes."

Ecaterina burst into laughter. "So is there anything else I can do for you?"

"I need someone to train against, though. He is so careful as if the training will break me. Holding back because I still need to learn more. You don't know any werebears do you?"

Ecaterina broke into giggles. "Oh, I do actually. Yes, indeed. My uncle happens to be one. Would you like me to ask him?"

Janna nodded eagerly "Yes. Please. It looks like Boris will be gone for another week. He has decided to see the refugees to the border before he returns. I want him to feel I am completely ready when he returns."

So Janna continued to train as a werebear against a werebear. Alexi couldn't deny his favorite niece's request. The women who supported Bethany Anne arranged for it to happen.

CHAPTER TWELVE

Refugee Column, Near the Mongolian Border

"Boris, a good morning to you," said Lev, approaching Boris's sleeping tent. The weather had been better for the last few days. Both Lev and Boris appreciated it, if for different reasons. Lev, because, despite everything, they would still make the rendezvous if a day late. Boris had confirmed the pickup would be there. Boris because it meant that ADAM could verify that no significant forces were moving to intercept.

The Mongolian Pack Mistress had sent a message. The first part of it was a slight rebuke to Boris for not asking for aid or giving her warning of the refugees. The Mongolian Pack, unlike most packs of the UnknownWorld, often had someone either inside the government or advising them directly. The Mongolian government and people were, at the moment, thrilled that the Chinese had been hammered. Although China was a major trade partner, historically they were seen as a threat.

Mongolia had no problem accepting the refugees

crossing their border but had no desire to make a great fanfare of it. With China weakened, Russia was now a more significant threat militarily. Still, Russia was out of position to do much to Mongolia, considering the existing tensions on its Western border with NATO and the Baltic States.

Also unusual was that the pack leader was female. It wasn't unheard of, but Sarangerel was an extraordinary woman. She and Boris had fallen out of contact since the fall of communism, and Boris knew the rebuke was for him going insular and quiet on her.

She had sought him out to train her when she decided, at the age of thirty, that she wanted to lead the Mongolian pack. At times in history, he had been forced to take over from a vicious or stupid pack leader who crossed Peter. The idea of having that region's pack leader indebted to him had a definite appeal. With Danislav and some of the other senior wolves assisting, he had tutored her not only in fighting but also in administration, law, and the Strictures.

She still owed him. While he probably should have sent a message to her, he had merely forgotten. He had sent the messenger back with apologies and an assurance that the refugees would not be there long. He reminded her that the Mongolians had walked the tightrope between hiding North Korean refugees and keeping positive relations with that nation successfully for years. Promising to discuss improving their communications with his oath-sworn leader, Boris had thought that the messenger's eyes would pop out in surprise.

After all, he had refused for centuries to swear an oath

to serve Peter. That was one thing that the Mongolian pack did know. For him to accept another as his leader was new and unsettling, he suspected.

When they crossed the border, Boris was at the head of the column. He saw a woman on horseback and smiled. Sarangerel had come to meet them personally.

"And how does the day treat you, Pack Mistress?" he asked her.

She scowled at him. "If there were not relatives between my pack and yours who thought to phone ahead, you would have me in an awful situation, Boris." She held her hands together in front of her, tapping the thumbs together. "What excuse do you have for me, Old Bear?"

"You'll probably meet my excuse when the pickup for my people arrives. I suspect she'll want to see them off."

Sarangerel's eye widened "I thought you were too much of another era to oath-swear to a female. Who is she anyway?"

His eyes darkened. "She is the woman who changed Michael, Sarangerel. That is all I needed to know about her. The devotion that her followers show her was just the cream on the milk."

"You mentioned him a couple of times. My people still think he's somewhat of a myth, you know."

Boris grabbed her down off her horse in a rapid movement. He shook her gently. "Don't, whatever you do, say that to Bethany Anne. She lost him a few months ago. He now lies with the heroes. In his death, he prevented hundreds from being killed by a nuke, including myself. Swear to me you will not bring him up in front of her! I will not have you cause her pain, Sarangerel."

Sarangerel was startled, and a bit frightened, although her only sign of that was a subtle widening of her eyes. She had never seen Boris take such an action. What had been meant to be a passing comment had invoked fear in him. Real fear. "Yes, Boris. I understand," she said, placing her hands in placation on his wrists. They tightened even more on her shoulders, so she added, "I swear I will not bring it up unless absolutely necessary."

Boris released her shoulders "What do you mean 'Absolutely necessary'"

"China's Weres are up to something. I cannot get a read on it. You know how explaining them, and their attitudes might bring up their general contempt for Michael and his children. They barely accepted Peter's punishments and believed Michael to be a boogieman invented by Peter to keep them under control. Your staunch support of Peter and the number of times you defeated their attempts at expansion was all that kept them in check. Now they are moving…"

"They will receive the same option my Czarina gave China's government. Try to kill me, sue for peace, or die. You will not have the luxury the Mongolian pack has so often taken between me and their provocations, Sarangerel. With Bethany Anne, if you are a part of the UnknownWorld, you are on her side, or you will be hunted and eliminated. Neutrality will not be a solution for you, especially if you don't want me to challenge for your pack and absorb it. Bethany Anne may not see it as I do, but the storm is coming. It is almost upon us. I will not leave any but allies at her back."

Sarangerel was shocked. This was her teacher. He had

taught her that unless the situation was most dire, neutrality was the best option. He truly believed such great changes were coming to make that threat.

She lowered her head in submission.

Boris turned and saw a black pod dropping from the sky. The two watched in silence as it stopped and hovered a few feet above the ground. Boris was surprised to see Dan open the hatch and wave to him. "Boris, Janna asked for some help from a more experienced interrogator. They have a live one apparently. So Bethany Anne sent me to pick you up and help. Come on."

Boris bowed slightly to Sarangerel, "It seems other duties call. I hope to talk to you later, student." He turned and hurried to the pod.

CHAPTER THIRTEEN

Command Container, Siberia

The pod landed two kilometers away from the container. If there was a chance that the Russians could localize the radar signature of the pod, there was no point in making the task easier for them.

"So what is so important that you were called in? I know I don't like rigorous interrogation techniques, but if you are getting a site or location, you can confirm it. If it's a ticking clock situation same deal. I have done it in the past. Besides, how did they get their hands on him?" Boris asked.

"Which question do you want to be answered first?" Dan responded with a grin.

"How they got him."

"Well, they received some intelligence from one of the groups. It seems that he had a cover job as security for a brothel. One of the regular visitors came in on a set schedule accompanied by two guards in uniforms with NVG flashes. So Janna went in as if she were looking for work. After knocking out the brothel owner, she killed the two guards and with our man's help left the building with the visitor. He was threatening her with how she'd be tortured when his boss came to retrieve him. Danislav helped her get him back to the command container."

"Since it isn't moving anytime soon, outside of an emergency, the entrenched team has moved the beds to the side of the container and set up tents and camouflage netting for more concealment. Inside of all of that, they've left the captive chained to a chair most of the day. A heavy, metal chair. Paul wanted to interrogate him immediately, but instead, Janna has been questioning him eighteen hours a day for three days straight. She's pulled a lot of information out of him. Apparently, the leader is a *man with terrifying eyes* called Konrad."

Boris's face took on a grim cast. He knew of only one vampire with that name. One of David's children. Boris had personally killed two of his brothers in the Great Patriotic War which complicated things. It meant there might be a personal aspect to this whole situation. Vampires could plan for centuries before taking revenge. Peter had assured Boris he had not revealed his identity to anyone but Michael, but could it have slipped out somehow?

Then he suddenly realized a part that was just as worrying. Janna had gone through the mission practically alone.

His eyes were stretching wide, Boris started immediately to bitch, "What in the nine hells were those diaper wearing dipstick fuckers thinking? Letting her go on a mission like that with practically no backup? It was too dangerous. I swear I will find a way to make my displeasure known about their ill-judged, reckless..." Boris's rant was interrupted by a chuckle from Dan.

"You have it bad, Boris," he said.

Boris stopped his tirade to stare at Dan. "What do you mean?"

"You are in love, my friend." He held up his hand to forestall Boris. "I've seen this reaction from a Were before. When Ecaterina told Nathan that she wanted to be part of active operations, he hit the ceiling. Get it under control before you see her. Otherwise, it will get messy. I reviewed the mission, and the plan was solid. They had an inside man, who has gone to ground, by the way. He was in far more danger than Janna. She's capable and a Werebear now. The job was a piece of cake."

Boris blinked. After actually listening to Dan and thinking for a minute, he realized that Dan was right. But that only brought up another problem. With a hint of despair in his voice, he asked "What am I going to do? It isn't appropriate for me to be in a relationship with my second-in-command. I'll have to request a..."

Dan interrupted again. "As long as you don't let it affect your job, Bethany Anne won't care. Think about it. Nathan and Ecaterina, John and Jean Dukes, Stephen and Jennifer, although don't you mouth a word about that last couple. If Bethany Anne thinks I let that slip, my ass is grass. Just keep doing your jobs and it won't be a problem."

Dan paused and considered his next recommendation, "I think you need to go talk to her when we get there. I can work over the man with Paul or Danislav, and if we still aren't getting anywhere we'll call for a bear, and one of you can change and see what that does to loosen his tongue. If pain doesn't work, fear might be just the tool we need."

Boris shook his head. "Ask Paul. He has some experience. Sometimes we've had to convince a Forsaken's human lackey to give him up. Paul figured out early on how much I disliked it, so he offered to take the task. He doesn't enjoy it but views it as sometimes necessary. Danislav finds it nearly as distasteful as I do."

When they entered the container, it was to see Paul making a production of laying down and hanging plastic around the chair to which the prisoner fastened. He looked up to Dan and Boris and said "Okay boss, ready to go in a minute or two. Wasn't expecting you quite yet. Just give me a bit more time, so the cleanup is easier. "

Dan caught on quickly and answered "Sure. Janna, your methods didn't work, so why don't you take a walk with Boris? He needs to get the bear ready in case I need it. I'm not blaming you, but this rigorous stuff takes a different edge is all. You pulled a fair amount out of him your way. Now, because he's a stubborn ass, I was sent. So we do it my way."

Paul looked at the prisoner and treated him to a vicious grin. "I've got the assistant covered, Janna. Just help Boris prepare the bear, will ya? One way or another, we'll probably need 'im. Either to clean up the corpse or to start at this fellow's tootsies if he stays stubborn."

Dan took a pair of leather gloves out of his pocket "Yes. We need to find out where this Konrad is, after all."

Boris and Janna left. Janna was a little confused, and once they were out of earshot she asked "Is it really necessary? I mean, it might get us the information faster than I could, but I was hoping for one of those that can force the truth out. Like Bethany Anne did to me."

Boris shrugged "They were all busy I'd imagine. Dan used to assist in operations to take out Forsaken vampires. I'm sure this isn't his first interrogation. Besides, not all vampires can do what you want. I imagine they are mostly busy, which is why they sent Dan. I have faith that he will be able to tell if someone is telling the truth or not. Vampire or not, he has the experience."

Paul finished hanging the plastic. He started pulling out a few things. A circular saw, a chisel, and hammer and finally a cricket bat.

Dan looked them over, lifting an eyebrow in query. Paul shrugged and explained, "I haven't got everything I'd like, but we can make do with this. It would be better to have a dentist on hand, to be honest. For some reason, having teeth drilled without anesthetic gets most people talking. I have one dentist on the way, but the sooner we get the information, the sooner we can act."

Dan pointed to the bat, "Why the cricket bat? I've always preferred a solid Louisville Slugger."

"A baseball bat is for amateurs. Look at who uses them most often. Criminals, like the mob. You can do more with a cricket bat." Paul turned to the man tied to the chair. His knee was conveniently clear of the arms. "You see, you can cause pain without permanent incapacitation." He swung the flat of the bat against the knee. The prisoner screamed once, but there wasn't the sound of breaking bones. "Or you can permanently damage them." He swung the bat edgewise at the knee. There was a solid crunch of breaking kneecap. The screams, this time, lasted a lot longer. "Besides, there are what, three or four countries where baseball is more popular than cricket? So you usually have more access to a cricket bat." Dan thought Paul's reasoning was impeccable, but the argument might unnerve the prisoner.

Dan pantomimed swinging an American baseball bat, "There's just something more balanced about a baseball bat. It's more comfortable to use."

Paul shrugged his shoulders, not giving an inch to Dan's argument, "It's all in practice, mate. You get used to it pretty quickly once you begin."

Dan turned to the prisoner. "You know, we can just keep going until you volunteer the information. My boss even gave me some stuff to heal up things like that so we can go again and again. Your choice."

The prisoner spat on the floor "I do not fear you as much as I do Konrad. You have no idea what I've seen him do."

"What? Let me guess. Drink the blood outta someone's neck when they failed him? Rip off someone's arm? Yeah, I have a fair idea. I've been fighting people like him for more than twenty long-ass years." Considering how much younger than his real age he appeared, there was no need to disrupt the interrogation by saying he had hunted them for thirty years.

Paul swung the flat against the other knee and ignored the screams, waiting a few seconds for them to die down before he turned to Dan "Only twenty? Damn, I've been doing it for twenty-five." The prisoner was trying to keep his sobs down, but failing miserably.

The prisoner looked shaken "You are just humans. I've seen a man change into a wolf. Another into a leopard. Nothing you can do will scare me."

Paul said conversationally. "Oh, I didn't know cats were possible. I mean Boris there can turn into a nine-hundred kilo bear, but a cat is a new one on me."

Dan grunted "There are rumors. Never seen one myself. Still, I think a bear is scarier. I mean fuck, Boris was flipping trucks on the last combat mission I went on." He turned to the prisoner "You know that refinery that your boys were guarding? It only took two of us to take them out. Me and Boris. That was it. If that's the best your Konrad can throw at us, I'm not really worried. There were ten wolves in that group - they went down like wheat at reaping time."

Paul chuckled and tapped the other knee with the flat of the bat again. Another set of screams. "So why did Bethany Anne send you?"

"Need to keep my skills sharp. If we can drag the info out of this spunking fuck knuckle." He held out his hand for the bat and drove it into the prisoner's groin. A scream with some sobbing ensued. "After all, when we hit space we might need to resort to torture. We're fairly sure we'll be able to tell if someone is lying. But forcing it out of them like she can on humans? We just don't know. And most skills tend to fall by the wayside if you don't use them."

Paul turned to their prisoner, "You ready to talk yet? I'm enjoying the workout, but if you wanna talk, then I'm happy to pause for a bit. At least, if it is the truth coming out of your mouth."

The prisoner looked at him, a mix of mild fear and great hatred in his eyes. His mouth remained firmly shut.

"Well, looks like we keep going with the workout." Paul slapped the guy across the face. "I'm sure once the dentist starts you'll talk, but we may as well keep having our fun."

Boris looked at Janna. Really looked at her. After more than a week of large meals and steady exercise, her body had filled out. (A little bird called Nathan had told him about Alexi training Janna while he was away.) Her original tall, willowy body was now slightly taller, with fuller hips, and a perfectly fantastic gait.

He found it hard to concentrate around her. When he closed his eyes, he could think of how much he liked and respected her. Her input on military matters was well-founded, and her intelligence was impressive. However, when he saw her, smelled her, his body took over. The sway of her ass was mesmerizing. Her long red-blonde hair was entrancing. His hormones and attraction collided with his respect for her abilities until he could not seem to think objectively.

Trying to find some balance, he attempted to think objectively. Her bust was, honestly, larger than he usually found physically attractive. That made no difference to his thoughts or feelings. He had learned over the past four hundred years that it was the person, not the body that was truly important. And she was an entrancing, intoxicating person to him on multiple levels. To his head, heart, and hormones.

The two of them both started talking at the same time. Janna broke off in a burst of laughter that sounded like sweet-toned bells. "You first," she said with a smile on her face.

He drew her into a hug and said "I think my time away has given me some perspective. Janna, if you are willing, I would like to see where 'us' will head. No pressure, beyond doing our jobs as well as we have been. But I missed you, worried about you horribly, while I was gone. When I found out what you had done while I was…"

She interrupted his sentence with a hungry, aggressive kiss. Breaking the touch of her lips on his, she laid a gentle finger to his mouth. "Don't spoil it by saying something like 'you were angry.' Or you wish I hadn't done it. It was simply part of the job. I will not have you saying what I can and cannot do, ignoring the fact that I am a grown woman." She waved her free hand up and down her body, illustrating her point. "A woman who has done this kind of work for five years. I was the best person to send. Danislav did object, so you know." She frowned, thinking about it, "Paul, if anything, encouraged me."

Boris shrugged and commented, "I am honestly not sure how Paul's brain really works. Even in the Unknown-World, many fear me. He never has. He is always pragmatic to the point of sociopathy when on a mission or a job."

"Balancing that, he shows a level of empathy with his family and friends many others cannot match. He is in many ways a cipher. Paul is only able to look at the pros and cons based on the mission requirements. He's never been able to look at the overall impact on an operation, though. Just the individual tasks. But he is brilliant in his work."

"I was going to say that after Dan had laughed at my reaction, I was forced to look at the mission pragmatically. You were right to go, and I am proud that you did so with success and flair. I am proud of you and your abilities."

He kissed her on the forehead, and she dragged him down into a hug and a deeper kiss. They lost all sense of time locked in each other's scent, kiss, and embrace.

After they had proved to the prisoner that they were willing to heal his injuries and go back again to the interrogation, he was more willing to talk. The nanite-infused liquid that Bethany Anne and TOM had provided to Dan increased the agony of the repeated questioning and proved a painful point. They obviously were happy to keep going, and Paul's repeated references to a dentist and the supposed timeline had an intensified effect.

Janna and Boris were broken out of their enjoyment of each other by Paul calling out to them "He's singing like a bird! I think you want to hear this, Boris."

The broken man gave descriptions of the three sites that Konrad used to base his operations and admitted that there was somewhere in the north near Finland that Konrad spent time. They also found out that Konrad had various Weres captured on these bases and was using them to improve his most loyal followers. With a success rate of about one in ten. Apparently, he didn't want to create a potential competitor as powerful as he was. Once they had the locations and grid references, ADAM did his magic. They confirmed that one was serving as a comms node, and was, therefore, the most likely place for Konrad to be at this time.

Paul was all for organizing a full press assault on the base. Boris and Danislav were not precisely against this, but agreed that there should be a better solution. Dan left them discussing it, since he didn't have a good handle on the capabilities of Boris's people. Besides, he needed to get back and report. Things were showing signs of breaking loose in too many places for him to be comfortable spending time away from the base in Australia unnecessarily. Boris had things well in hand here.

Bottom line, though, events in Russia still had the potential to go so completely FUBAR that he needed to report to Bethany Anne and start contingency planning.

After Dan had left, discussions changed to how to draw forces out from the base by staging a closely-fought ambush on a convoy within twenty kilometers of the base. At worst, it would pull a portion of the guard force that could be the real ambush target. At best, Konrad would come himself.

CHAPTER FOURTEEN

NVG Base Omega, Central Siberia, Russia

Shen was becoming unnerved by his captor's weird behavior. He had expected more questions and visits after the earlier incident. What was unexpected was for the vampire to move his office into the same room as Shen's cell. The considering looks he'd been getting were not a comfort either, although the increased rations were.

Konrad had alternated between ranting about his dead brothers and their killer, the curious site discovered near Archangelsk, and real plans on how to maneuver his political group into shifting Russia's policies to align with Konrad's own objectives. At least once every three days, he would rant at how gallingly effective the commander of the raiders and his troops were against his forces. He did not realize how paranoid he sounded when he blamed the attacks on Boris.

Konrad had given Shen all his reports on the attacks and what he had been able to piece together of the attacks on the supply convoys. The vampire had started to assign a company of troops as convoy escorts, and the raids had died back, only to be replaced by spoiling attacks on the bases.

Whoever was organizing the raiders was brilliant in many ways. All the NVG he had seen were on edge as if they were expecting an attack at any moment. Shen knew it was wearing on them, and tired people made more mistakes.

From the reports and the limited history, he knew that the raids could be originating from Boris. Or they could be a new faction of Chechens, as many indicators in the reports suggested. It could be some other foreign or domestic group that wanted everyone to think that it was the Chechens. There was not enough data. None of the raiders who had been killed or injured had been left on site. There was the occasional scrap of a torn uniform, but those could have come from anywhere, even if it was the camouflage pattern and color combination favored by the Chechen rebels.

While Shen was reading over the latest reports, Andrev came running into the room and saluted Konrad, "Sir, we have received reports that the convoy that was due today has come under attack and is pinned, but holding ground." Shen's ears almost twitched at this. If the irregular troops were commanded by Boris, this was almost certainly a trap. The big Were could probably defeat Konrad, but Shen remained quiet. With incomplete information, he could hardly be expected to voice possibilities or advice, let alone a warning.

If Boris killed Konrad, it was entirely possible that he would come to the base. Although Shen feared the outcome if Boris found him here, he feared it far less than any reasonable result of remaining trapped in this base with the unstable vampire. The man was riding the ragged edge of insanity, almost ready to tip over into full madness. Shen knew that being a madman's prisoner was not likely good for one's long-term health.

So Shen kept his suspicions to himself while the vampire and his command team planned a reaction force to 'smash' the ambush. They had convinced themselves that Omega base was their second most secret location. So to them, it seemed more likely that an organization discovering it would keep looking and find the Archangelsk base. With the secrecy surrounding that location, it would appear to be the actual HQ.

Omega base was a centralized comms node, but they were careful to keep the traffic hidden and relayed through other bases. A reasonable person would conclude it was an important site, but any attack was, in their analysis, more likely to be directed against Archangelsk.

Shen thought their analysis showed why he was glad that he was their prisoner, not one of their men or officers. Rather than positing a scenario into which the facts slotted neatly, they were twisting and bending many of their facts to fit their situation. When he was asked his opinion, he responded simply, "It fits as well as anything I can come up with. There are other possibilities, but this is as likely or more likely than most of them."

Andrev nodded with a vicious smile. "Good. Now we have a chance of knocking these raiders back on their heels. If we can hand them a defeat, it can only weaken their resolve."

Konrad nodded slowly. "Yes. Ready the HQ guard squad as well. We will lead the rescue effort, and make sure some of the raiders escape. With our appearance, we can spread fear among these troublemakers. They may work for Boris, but I doubt he risked revealing his other forms to them for oh-so-many reasons. They may not even realize the base is in such close proximity, in which case this additional force will break the strength of the raiders we attack by the shock and surprise alone. Their leaders will appear less competent, and that will erode their resolve and morale. Go, Andrev. Gather the forces. We will need to leave only a handful of survivors. I will go prepare myself."

CHAPTER FIFTEEN

Relief Force Ambush Site, 20 Kilometers from NVG Base Omega

Boris had been forced to place most of the Weres he'd been able to gather for this operation with the group ambushing the convoy. They would act as both a reserve and a TARFU plan. If this strategy was unsuccessful, at least the original ambush force would be able to get out. The force attacking the convoy numbered two hundred riflemen and fifty Weres. They had already taken more casualties than he liked, but were doing a good job of pinning the convoy in place. It made them a tempting target for any relief force, and one was already forming in the NVG base along this road. He'd placed Danislav in charge of that part of the offensive.

This attacking force had a dozen mortars, a handful of anti-armor weapons and twenty of his snipers with Barretts. He had three carefully hoarded anti-vehicle mines on the road, as well as a demolition charge. Only a thousand men had been able to be gathered for the second force, and it worried him. Still, he had the Ace that hadn't been used. Bethany Anne had eight Black Eagles on standby. She'd also cleared and dropped off the Spetsnaz that had defected or been captured by the refugees. Two of them had been willing to carry out the brutal orders against the refugees without the implied threat of being killed by their more ruthless comrades. The pair had been executed by the rest of the willing defectors. The rest had arrived earlier and were acting both as observers and poised to disrupt any retreat by the relief forces.

Boris had contempt for Konrad's open and easily-disrupted plan. The bases the vampire had built or secured gave him enormous strategic reach but were too dispersed to support each other. They were tactically vulnerable. This was true even if four of them provided jump-off points to nuclear sites.

Tactically, they were at least two days apart from each other. Against the mobile forces of the Russian military, the best the vampire could do would be to pull off ambushes to slow consolidated troops down, while he gathered enough soldiers to force a confrontation. Against spoiling attacks and convoy raids like Boris used, Konrad could not even block and stop possible escape routes. Without forces gathered in large groups, the skirmishers of the Were's forces would be impossible to block or avoid. Several bases were large enough to assist, but even fully-manned their effectiveness would be limited since the NVG had no helicopter or air support.

Perhaps they had planned on using the massacre of the Regressive Whites who had been 'plotting against the President' to speed their recruitment. If they had spun it deftly, it might have worked, enabling them to recruit large numbers of ex-military into their ranks. That did not even consider the rumors they could spread that would have attracted many of the garden-variety thugs. *Loot a town under the guise of suppressing those who wish to topple the government* would have been a great draw for those types of criminals.

It didn't matter what Konrad's plans had been. Through luck, Boris had delayed them. If it held, he would end those plans tonight.

Konrad was likely to lead his men personally. An attack on his forces this close to his base was a personal affront he could not ignore. He'd lead from the front, so Boris had to as well. All the troops had magazines pre-loaded with sintered metal and silver ammunition. A fifth of them had those magazines already seated in their rifles. They would not be as effective against humans, but it was a necessary precaution against a force that had previously shown it had some Weres incorporated into its ranks.

The Spartans (as Boris had designated his small Spetsnaz force) reported that a column of trucks was moving out of the base towards the ambush site. That was something of a relief to Boris, although it made a lot of sense tactically. His forces had shown proficiency with anti-armor weapons and, since the battle north of Romanovka, had used no booby traps or prepared explosives. The number of APCs that they had taken out had to be hurting the NVG. Those couldn't be cheap, even if they were getting post-service discards. He was lucky they didn't seem to have tanks. But political troops such as the NVG rarely had armor or artillery. For them, it was a numbers game as often as not.

Boris checked his position again. His original body armor for both forms he had passed on to Janna when Alecta sent him a new set that she and ADAM had designed together. Janna had checked that it didn't restrict her too much. She had insisted he wear the newer armor over every objection he raised. The new armor had overlapping plates that would spread to provide more effective protection in his Pricolici form. She also knew she was to keep clear of Konrad. Her skills had improved rapidly, but he doubted there was another Were who could take on a third generation Vampire like Konrad. Peter and Nathan together probably could, but that was it as far as he knew. Janna's assignment was to cover his back from Weres and would be supported by Paul.

Paul had opted to wear a relatively thick ceramic-insert vest. He was the base of fire, or designated shooter, for the pair of them anyway. It was their job to protect him and his to shoot the head off any other Weres in their area. That was why he would be firing single shots tonight, to make sure that the attackers that came close to his friends did not survive.

Boris heard the trucks moving down the road towards them. It was probable the infantry was planning on dismounting a couple of klicks from the ambush and coming in on foot. Without APCs, that was the only logical action. He really hoped that Konrad was in the lead truck, but he doubted he would be that lucky, especially when he saw the fourth vehicle in the line. It had armor plates on its side. That was where the vampire would be. He could smell the odor of old, rotting blood coming from the column now, and was sure Konrad was in it. He was unlikely to have tried for deception on a rescue mission, even if his arrogance and ego would allow it.

The lead truck rolled over one of the mines and practically disintegrated, throwing its load of men outward in a bloody spray of body parts. There were yells from the column as the remaining seven hundred troops quickly exited the vehicles. They were moving far more smoothly than those that had been ambushed weeks ago. It looked like they had been practicing responses, or had training beyond what the first group had received. This was going to get bloody quickly. He just hoped that there were enough doses of the nanites to keep the fatal casualties down.

He heard a group of howls coming from the back of three of the trucks. That made things worse. At least thirty, probably more like fifty, werewolves. It was time to change. He nodded to Janna and picked up the AA-12. About ten werewolves were charging in his direction as he transformed. Once his sight cleared he saw that the wolves were concealed by a cloud in his mind. He knew that Konrad wasn't as powerful as Michael. This must be a trick he'd thought up. Still, concealment wasn't cover. He held down the trigger on his AA-12 and emptied the thirty-round drum of silver coated buckshot into the cloud, hoping to hit as many as possible. He was grimly satisfied when he heard four yelps and some cursing in German. He'd managed to at least hit the bastard. That left six that would be worrying more about him and Janna than the silver burning in their bodies.

He saw four head for Janna. Poor decision. With her training, six may not have been enough, but when one dropped to half-dozen steady cracks from Paul's rifle, he knew she would be fine. There was not a werebear he knew of that couldn't take at least three wolves. Not anymore.

The mental mist moved closer to him at an increased speed as he ripped the long hilted gladius from its sheath and let loose an unearthly roar. One of the remaining wolves lunged for his throat. He caught it in the air with his free paw and crushed its chest, throwing the body as hard and far as he could. In the background, he heard the steady, distinct cracks of Paul's Steyr AUG over the sounds of other combat. The sharp snaps of grenades detonating filled his ears, while the smells of the battlefield, of blood and ruptured bowels assaulted his nose. The stink of shit and urine from the inexperienced combat troops who hadn't known to make appropriate actions before the battle lent a sour note to the odor of wet dog and human.

The stink of old blood coming from in front of him got stronger. Apparently, his fight with the first Were to attack him had made the remaining wolf and Konrad more cautious.

Suddenly, Boris felt a sharp burning in the back of his neck. Swearing as the combined aroma of leopard and human reached his nose. He realized that the existence of the werecat among Konrad's forces had been mentioned in the interrogation of the vampire's officer.

Where he had found one willing to serve with him, the fates only knew. Boris reached one hand back and grabbed the far smaller Were by the scruff of the neck. Pulling hard, the cat was forced to choose between losing a large chunk of skin and flesh, or loosening its grip on him. It opted to let go. He swung his arm and sent it flying through the air.

Janna was having no problem with the three wolves left to attack her. One had tried to hamstring her early on in the fight before the others were in position. She had quickly spun around and bitten its head clean off in a bloodlust she had not felt before. This was new to her and she found it exhilarating. She quickly spun back around to face the other two. They tried to split her attention by circling in opposite directions, but she had trained against this tactic and feinted towards one. As soon as it leaped backward, she turned to maul the other with her claws as it rushed in to hamstring her. The last wolf grasped the danger it was in too late. Paul had drawn a bead on the exposed head, and the werewolf went down with a pair of bullets through the skull.

She heard a roar of pain from Boris, followed shortly by a snarl from some large cat. She turned to see Paul go down with a grunt and a groan as the cat eviscerated his belly through his armor. Shards of useless protection ripped, almost exploding into the air, but he managed to stay conscious and focused enough to pull his .50 caliber revolver. There were five thunderous blasts as he emptied it into the leopard.

Something tore inside Janna as she saw Paul collapse in front of her, barely breathing, and blood trickling down Boris's back. Her love was severely injured, and her friend was down. As that something broke, a great rage filled her, and her body changed. Transforming into a form about which she had been cautioned about, Janna turned, filled with the strength, rage, and power of this new shape. Uninjured, she charged the werecat that was limping on three legs. It tried to flee, but her paw-hand slammed down on its skull, crushing it beneath her retribution, her sorrow. The body fell limply to the earth, slight twitches causing shudders and a small semblance of life as it succumbed to death. She turned and saw Paul struggling with one of the nanite needles as one of the nearby soldiers came to his aid. There was nothing more she could do, but avenge his pain on as many of the NVG as she could find.

She had seen a broken rib sticking out of his chest and his gaping belly wound. It did not seem likely he would survive. Even with the nanites in his body, they were not the miracle he needed.

That he was still conscious was.

That made her decision to rejoin the fight easy. She just needed to kill as many of these *zmei gorinichi pizda* as she could. Two of the Weres who had been shot seemed to have removed the silver buckshot from their wounds. Moving before they could avoid her, she knocked one of them to the ground and pounded it with her foot as she reached for the other. Grabbing the second, she dragged it to her mouth, ignoring its futile struggles, ripped its head off, chewed, and swallowed.

The two remaining injured beasts froze in terror and stopped trying to remove the silver. They started to hobble off away from her as fast as they could. Boris was frightening, but his eyes showed control. All they could see in her eyes was incandescent rage. Fury at what had happened in this battle perhaps, but also an anger at what these pizda had been trying to do to her country. Her wrath had finally exploded from the confines she had placed around it and boiled to the surface in a geyser of blood and pain.

She waded into the combat, ignoring bullet hits time and again, as she stalked like a bestial goddess of nature through the NVG troopers. Realizing that their fire was useless, many of them tried to flee. They were not fast enough. Rather than the lumbering gait one would expect from such a giant creature, she moved with a startling light-footed grace and speed.

Even Boris's forces found it disconcerting. Seeing what had to be a thousand kilograms of a cross between a bear and a human was disturbing. Seeing it move with the grace of a dancer and the fury of a mother bear defending her cubs was downright terrifying.

Even for those likely to fall in the cub category.

Boris kept his focus on Konrad. A moment of distraction may be all that this man needed to kill or critically injure him. While he heard her roar and her form crossed his vision, he cursed internally. That slight distraction was all that Konrad had needed. He felt a slight burn across his leg as a knife dug in. He mauled the vampire's shoulder, but he could not afford to trade blow for blow with a vampire. Michael had taught him that.

With the pain he had caused Konrad, the mist dropped. He could clearly see that he had only hit the vampire with a half dozen shots on one leg. Without the same weakness against silver as a Were, that was barely a scratch. Although Boris's wounds were healing, he was now at a disadvantage. He still faced off against an uninjured Were and Konrad.

"Why diiid youuu attaccck my people, Konrrrad?" he growled out.

Konrad smiled viciously and purred, "Why not? All these humans are cattle, are they not? Can't you see that? Are you that blind? They had a reputation I could use to gather support. A shame you intervened."

Boris responded with a scowl "Cattllle? Nooo Konrrrad, they are People. Indiiiivvviduuuals. Not Playthiiings. Not Cattllle. Cattlle cannot figgght back. Evvven if we trriied to taake charrge we would faiil. What we belong asss isss Guarrrdians. Not rrulerrs."

"That is a philosophy that will get you killed one of these days, old Bear. You are not strong enough to protect them from me. I turned my brothers, they were weaker than I. David turned me. You will find me far superior to them."

"Perrrhaaps," Boris responded calmly.

At this moment, perhaps thinking the conversation had distracted him, the Were lunged for Boris' leg. A flick of the blade in his hand sent the wolf's head rolling. The rest of the wolf continued into Boris with a wet thump. It didn't even budge him. The vampire, perhaps hoping the Were had distracted Boris in turn, charged. He drove one clawed hand toward the bear's guts and the other at the neck. Boris batted the lower attack away with the sword, slicing into Konrad's flesh. The Werebear grabbed and held the other hand, crushing it in his fist. The crackle of shattering bones was loud in the air, as pain crossed Konrad's face. Boris hurled him away as Konrad's other hand reached for his neck.

Konrad somersaulted in the air to land on his feet. He

felt concern, as the hunger rose in him, greater than he had felt for years. Hearing the whine of one of the injured wolves just behind him, the vampire reached out with his still functional hand and grabbed it. He bit down into its neck and drank deeply. The surge of energy and returning feeling to his injured hand heartened him. He could still win this, even though Boris was far stronger than he had expected.

For a short time, the two combatants tested each other, feinting and dodging, but Boris grew bored with this. He now had the measure of the man and knew that he could take him down the next time the circling action was reversed.

Konrad didn't even see the blow that landed on his shoulder as he changed his direction of movement. The blow drove him to his knees, and he felt the snap of his shoulder breaking under the force. Another blow landed on his side, crushing his ribcage. His eyes flashed red as the hunger consumed him. The vampire barely managed to evade Boris' blow but managed to grab the Were's arm as it went past. He turned, and reflexively bit down on Boris' wrist and drank, desperate for the blood within and the energy it would give him.

It would be the last mistake he would make. Boris's free hand reached out, grabbed the vampire's neck and snapped it. His other arm, still dripping some blood, grabbed the hair on Konrad's head. Reaching down he picked up his short sword and swung it in a deadly arc, cleanly decapitating Konrad.

With a fierce bellow, he proclaimed his victory. At the

sound of another monster on the field, the remaining NVG broke, to be slaughtered by their ambushers.

Boris turned to look at Paul. Two of his medics were working on the sorely wounded man, but when one of them glanced up, he shook his head slightly. It did not look good. Tired and bleeding, Boris lumbered over to his friend.

One of the medics looked at him and whispered, "We've already given him two doses of nanites. He's stable now, but I don't see him staying that way. The wound across the stomach isn't healing fast enough. And we are out of doses with all the other casualties. We've picked out all the ceramic fragments and cleaned it but…"

Boris thought carefully. If Janna was here, between them, they might be able to give him enough of their blood to get him to a pod, and Bethany Anne's medical unit. But she was in a rage. Until she wore it out, it was not likely that she would return. He thought to Janna, *Please come back. Paul needs you!*

He was completely stunned when he heard a response. *What? Who is this?*

He concentrated again, *Janna, it's Boris. We might be able to save Paul, but I need you here.*

The silence was his only answer.

Soon afterward, he felt the ground shuddering slightly as she pounded back to where they had started the battle.

He held Paul's hand, saying, "Stay with me old friend."

He heard a mumbled response, "No' goin' anywhere boss. 'Lecta would 'ill me."

Boris made an anguished decision. Placing his still-healing wrist near Paul's mouth, he ripped the scab off and let the blood flow. Positioning his arm so that the blood dribbled into Paul's mouth, Boris said, "Drink, old friend. You'll feel better." Paul drank deeply and lapsed into unconsciousness.

Janna looked at what Boris had done and grabbed a knife between a thumb and index finger. Carefully, she cut her wrist and dripped the blood across the gut wound. With the broken bone injuries already straightened and probably healing, the gaping stomach wound was the only logical place for her to help.

Over the next half hour, Paul's breathing strengthened. His stomach wound sealed and seemed to be healing at an accelerated rate.

Looking up, Boris saw Bethany Anne approaching with Ashur dogging her steps, on the lookout for unknown danger. "Why didn't you ask for air support earlier, you walking fur coat? We could have taken out the entire column…"

"And perhaps compromised any chance of a positive relationship with Russia. If that had happened, the Russian civilian deaths would be far more than we lost today? We have what, a hundred or so dead on our side?" He apparently did not think the NVG dead counted in this equation. In truth, they didn't. Either way, they would have died.

"You would have ended up killing far more than that in Russia's military. Those men gladly gave their lives to prevent that. I do have one request, though." He pointed to Paul. "Please, take him to your medical device. And have Alecta near him when he wakes. We had to give him much of our blood to save him, and I fear the potential consequences for him."

Bethany Anne glanced at Paul and muttered loud enough for them to hear, "You antiquated excuse for an ambulatory, moth-eaten bear rug! Of course." She walked over to Paul, put one hand on him, the other reaching for Ashur, and all three of them disappeared.

CHAPTER SIXTEEN

<u>Near NVG Base Omega, Russia</u>

The fleeing and broken men fled the combat, trying to put the frightening battlefield behind them. The Spartans wisely chose not to block the routed force since it outnumbered them heavily, and because the panicked soldiers showed no signs of regrouping. Instead, Boris' new allies moved aside and merely observed, making sure that no officer was attempting to rally a return.

Personal interviews with some of Boris' vampire allies had convinced the Spartans that they had some idea of what might cause these men to flee. After talking to Boris, they felt prepared for the appearance of his 'other form.' It was still a significant shock when a seven-and-a-half-foot tall human-bear hybrid emerged with deadly grace from the woods. Especially when it was not Boris, but Janna. Even knowing that the monster drawn from their childhood nightmares was on their side did not lessen the awe or reduce the fear.

They were glad when she turned back to the main battlefield.

Evgeni was getting used to the first name and rank that Boris preferred. He turned to Sergeant Yosif, and said, "I've never felt relief at an ally leaving before." Yosif only shrugged.

"Better on our side than theirs, sir," he replied laconically. "Sir, should we move back to the observation positions? Or move up towards the base? There are several abandoned trucks we could use as transport if we wanted, but if we overtake those sorry bastards, they might try something.

"Never seen anyone flee so hard before, not even those poor *pizda* slavers we ambushed last year. The ones whose *slaves* started castrating the wounded."

"On foot, I think, Yosif. There is no significant advantage for us in taking the trucks. Inform Danislav of the movement and our plans since he said something about supporting us after the main action."

The sergeant started barking orders in rapid succession, and within a couple of minutes, the Spartans were moving out. Evgeni was proud of how quickly his men responded and formed up. They had given him their best, and he was determined to be worthy of their loyalty.

Boris was exhausted. He'd spent the last ten minutes teaching Janna a calming exercise when she declined to change back to human in case she needed the power and ferocity of her current form to assault the base.

Don't lose yourself, my love. I could not bear the pain of that, he thought quietly to her.

I won't. I wonder why we can talk to each other this way, though, she replied.

That she was showing curiosity was a good sign. When the rage took over, all a person thought about was violence and the hunger.

You need to stay here, Boris. You've received enough wounds today. I only got a few nicks from lucky bullets. You were mauled quite badly.

Boris could feel the concern behind her thoughts. He waved her off. *Don't mother me. You're too young to do it convincingly. Take those willing to go with you. I will follow behind once the injured are loaded.*

He felt her smile like a soft brush on his mind, and she was gone. Janna had changed her focus to the mission, moving on to further action and battle. His acceptance and confidence in her strength provided him a small moment of joy before he turned his thoughts back to war.

About four hundred men had volunteered to assault the base if Danislav deemed it worth the risk. Boris' adopted son was still annoyed at having missed the big fight but had been partially placated by the command of the base assault force. It helped his attitude that one of the drones had caught the battle on camera so anyone that wanted could watch the action later. Boris was quite sure it would be popular viewing by many.

Still, Boris doubted that any formal attack on the base would be necessary. Another thousand of his troops would be filtering into the area within a day, so they could stand off and reduce the base then if they needed to without the chance of additional casualties. To increase the one-sided nature of the encounter, the mortars were on their way with the reserves. Without the vampire leading the base forces, Boris suspected many who had joined the NVG would disappear into the forest or surrounding villages.

With the NVG force shattered, he would be surprised if there were anyone left living on the base when he got there. Janna's appearance would spread the panic quickly, ensuring that those that had not already fled upon hearing of the death of their vampire leader and the decimation of the special Were troops would rapidly depart. Not one NVG Were had escaped, although they had caused forty of Boris' fatalities. A bitter toll, but lighter than it would have been without Bethany Anne's support on the logistical front.

He slowly got to his feet and went to assist those organizing the evacuation of the wounded from the area. Perhaps they didn't need to move far... not yet at least.

Janna was shocked when she approached the base. There was no defensive fire, in fact, there was nothing but silence. It looked like Evgeni was right. The fear of the routed thugs had spread to the base defenders, and the news of Konrad's defeat and death had caused widespread abandonment.

She had changed back to her human form when the main areas had been cleared and the defensive weaponry secured. Evgeni had been surprised and a little confused that it was her and not Boris. Janna promised to explain it later, which seemed to calm him.

Danislav had brought her pants along with him. She was relieved more than a little. Being one of less than fifty women and the only one that was half naked had been embarrassing, even if none of the men had looked at her inappropriately or commented.

They had two reasons to avoid any commentary she supposed. First, she could break any one of them over her knee. While that was scary enough, it didn't even approach what Boris was likely to do to them if he found out they had disrespected her.

She heard the trucks with the wounded and the remainder of their force approaching in the muted growl of engines. The vehicles passed a group that was organizing the dead for recovery and burial. This late in the autumn, it was best to just cover the bodies and set guards. It had already been decided to bury them in the Romanovka cemetery before they left.

Boris had jumped out of the lead truck before it was entirely stopped and immediately went to her.

"Have the buildings been cleared yet?" he asked

Janna replied, pointing to each of the buildings in turn, "The barracks, base hospital, and mess hall have all been checked along with the armory and towers. The main administrative building and base brig are being searched at this time by combined teams of Weres and Spartans."

Boris nodded and waved the convoy towards the base hospital that Janna had identified. The trucks moved obediently toward their target. With over eighty moderately wounded troops that had not been treated with nanites due to a supply shortage, the most lightly injured might end up in the barracks. Still, none of those were life-threatening or critical, so there was no reason for concern.

One of the Spartans came running from the administrative building toward them.

"Sir, Ma'am, we have found a man being held in one of the basement offices that had been converted to a cell and office combination. We thought it best to inform you immediately and ask how you wanted to deal with the situation."

Boris turned to Janna, who nodded. "Lead on. Maybe he knows something that could be useful to us."

When they entered, the odor of both old blood and unwashed human was overwhelming. It was evident that the man in the room was a prisoner. One that Konrad had, for whatever reason, felt was valuable, but was not controlled enough to let roam free. The prisoner looked a little gaunt as if he had not been receiving enough food. He had distinctive East Asian heritage but was taller and more muscled than typical of the area. His hair was a dark brown rather than the more prevalent black as well. After a few moments, they could detect the odor of a Werecat under the stronger smells.

Janna's attention was immediately drawn to the desk. Despite having a laptop on it, her focus was the folders on the surface. On top of the filing cabinets, on top of every flat surface in the 'office.' Folders and more folders. She opened the filing cabinet drawers to find even more files, most of which contained a mixture of printouts and hand-written notes. Showing obvious delight, her expression turned to disgust as she looked more closely. A variety of curses wafted around her like stinging bees.

"Goddamn, paranoid needle fucker," she muttered.

"What's wrong?" Boris asked.

"All of this is written in German or one of the Norse languages for starters. I know German but never studied the northern languages. Despite the ability to recognize them, I have not the capacity to translate anything in the language to something we can use. Even then much of it is in shortened forms that would take a team weeks to decrypt. Some of it also looks like code."

Boris looked at her incredulously. "Why is that a problem? Why would we need a team to decrypt them? We send them up the chain and get them to sort it," he said, very conscious of the prisoner's presence. He thought to her, *ADAM can probably help us there.*

She blushed at slipping into her past role and forgetting the resources available to her now.

The prisoner spoke up at this point. Softly and hesitantly he said, "Make sure you send the laptop with the papers then. He would often refer to it while writing. I suspect it has some of the code keys on it."

"Who are you anyway? What had you done to attract the attention of these motherless bastards and made them give you such palatial accommodations?" Boris asked with irony in his voice. Before Shen could answer, Boris raised a commanding hand, speaking with absolute steel in his voice. "Before you answer, I'll inform you now I want the truth and am feeling quite tired. Killing a powerful vampire is never easy. We will be checking the truth of your answers. But afterward, I will promise you at least a hot shower and a meal. Be aware, however, if you lie to us, it will be your last meal."

Shen was worn out. He had meant to gloss over his past, but it wouldn't be worth trying to fool the Ghost Bear. His reputation, as the saying went, preceded him. If he had defeated Konrad, as seemed likely given the situation, he was out of Shen's league. Konrad had made Shen feel like a kitten. Not that fighting was Shen's skill set.

"I was trading the location of a Soviet-era weapons cache for some quantum processors. Prototypes. When I turned up to make the deal, there was the smell of vampire. I was ambushed as I left and felt that changing in such a built-up location to escape was a bad idea. It was a painful discovery to find that the vampire was interested in me as an experimental subject. He'd take my blood at least once a week and try to make more werecats with it. Only had one success, a real shitjacker called Andrev.

"Between the pain and the boredom I was slowly going insane. When what I am assuming were your attacks started to be a problem, he gave me profiles of groups opposed to him and set me on pattern analysis. Basic stuff for a computer science major, especially since I've studied human to machine cybernetic interfacing. I concluded that you were a likely cause of his problems.

"He was convinced that if you were to attack one of his bases personally, it would be his research site near Archangelsk. His 'most secret' base he called it. I didn't voice it but given the pattern of your attacks, switching from higher risk to low risk, the attack on the convoy didn't make sense whether you knew the base was here or not. Unless it was a trap. I dodged the question when he asked me since I'd figured out by then he could tell when I was lying. So I took a chance. He'd already convinced himself and his second that they wipe out the raiding force. Then you found me here."

Boris looked at him thoughtfully and continued with his questions, "Your personal history?"

Shen looked uncomfortable. "My mother was a werecat who fell in love with a werewolf. Such couplings are taboo in China, so they fled to India. Dad runs a successful export business. I earn my way by representing the family enterprise. I do a few black market information deals on the side. Mom doesn't know, and Dad doesn't like it, but he accepts my choices. I think his attitude stems from how judgmental their families were. Maybe because he sees it as me making my own way in the world…"

Shen continued rambling through his family history for a few minutes. His exhaustion was evident, so Boris called in Danislav.

"Take him for a shower and some food. Put him in a clean prison cell. Two guards at all times, suicide watch. We'll need to take him with us. He might be useful, but we can't have an information seller out there with data on us to sell to the highest bidder. He'll probably sleep. Make sure the guards know if something happens to him before what he's told us is checked out they'll answer to me."

Boris turned and left, looking for a meal and bed himself.

CHAPTER SEVENTEEN

Hunting Cabin, Middle of Nowhere, Siberia

It had been a busy couple of months for Boris and his command group. Often they had to split into two groups, with Danislav leading one assault and Boris with Janna leading the other. Occasionally, four separate and simultaneous attacks occurred. Mopping up the outposts, bases and separated forces of the NVG had fallen to his group. The Russian military had been given the information, including that the group's leader had been a German citizen. Given the potential political fallout from this, a compromise had been negotiated between the military establishment and Boris.

The number of criminals and former criminals that had been found amongst the casualties by military analysis teams was above twenty-five percent. The NVG needed to be broken up before someone strong took the helm. The military was leery of doing it, as were the internal police forces and the Border Force. That left calling up the national guard, as it was their role in Russia, legally speaking, or using Boris's forces and calling it 'fighting amongst criminal elements.' He had agreed to take on that role if two conditions were met. The first was full clemency papers for every member of his group for the duration of the 'necessary actions for the security of the state.' The other was payment.

His group had provided enough of the papers and files to show that Konrad's intention was to use the NVG to force the government to dance to his tune. Boris could prove that despite Romanovka's history, they had never been a danger to the state. The NVG was. Some in the military were suspicious of his motives when he added two provisions to the deal. One was the monetary payment, which was about the same as it would have cost the military to mobilize units and neutralize the remaining NVG. The second was two suitable pieces of land surrounding bases of his choice to explore the repatriation and relocation of Romanovka's people if they so wished. Throughout the negotiations, he had implied that his forces were mercenaries who he was either paying himself or owed him favors.

Considering what had happened with China, who had accepted the refugees, not to mention other political concerns, they had decided not to press that point. Most of the military bases in question were in the east anyway. The Russian government was currently running a program giving land to foreigners to attract settlers to Siberia. So it wouldn't cost the state anything if the price of that property was rolled into the existing program.

In exchange for their graciousness, Boris had agreed to hand over any prisoners. He had made sure any Were amongst the NVG died in battle. They had all fought to the end, so it had not become an issue. The Weres knew the punishment Boris would exact for joining a group willing to commit mass murder. Better to die cleanly in battle had been their unanimous choice.

The exception was Shen, who remained with Boris' team. The Werebear commander had permitted him to let his parents know of his safety, so they didn't worry. After weeks of working on small projects, mostly cross-checking captured records for them, Shen seemed a comfortable fit within the team.

He was still, however, a prisoner with work that was important but always double-checked. Shen was an essential part of the eradication of Konrad's organization. It was vital that it be eradicated, rather than cutting its head off only to have it grow back like a hydra. He had ten guards assigned to him permanently, both for protection and control. Considering that Shen was now free to shower, eat whatever he wanted, and sleep in a proper bed, his living situation had improved tremendously. It was evident that he appreciated the improvement and was becoming more comfortable with the team itself.

Boris knew that it was not ADAM or Tom's fault that Janna had been almost killed, but it did not seem to calm his nerves anytime that he remembered the appearance of her unconscious body. His knowledge of the exceptional abilities that they represented could not overwhelm the protective instincts of a Were for his mate.

Boris thought about how the last few months had changed him, his relationships, and the world around him. Behind his closed eyelids, he mentally compared his world before Bethany Anne and now, smiling a bit in reminiscence. He opened his eyes after his thoughts returned to the present, realizing that they were nearly at their destination.

They had a dozen small outposts left to conquer and the one large base, the Archangelsk. If only they could figure out where it was located. Its precise geographic site had been absent from all the notes. ADAM and TOM had tried several methods to try and find it from orbit but to no avail. The scans hadn't picked up anything particularly of interest.

There was something peculiar about how Konrad had referenced the base, in every entry where he had written about it. Boris knew that there was something important there, something that teased his brain and tugged on his intuition. Bethany Anne agreed with him, knowing that it was important and feeling just as frustrated over their joint inability to locate it.

"Boris, stop that," Janna said sleepily as he kept going over things in his head. "You agreed with Danislav's choice of commanders to take out the recruiters and recruiting stations. When you go all analytical like that for long enough, it always wakes me up."

She snuggled her naked back against him. The contact of her warm form brought back other, pleasant, memories of the last two months. He had been both surprised and pleased that combat gave her an uncommon reaction. She had been demandingly affectionate when they had reached safety after each mission. Not that he was complaining. It had been gratifying, he thought. It was nice to have found someone with whom he could share all of his life, rather than fleeting moments that were edited carefully. Being able to just be himself gave him a freer feeling than he had ever had.

It was also something he had never really dreamed could be an option. His mother's warning against turning someone had pretty much ruled that out for him. He had never found a female vampire to his taste since many of them were among the Forsaken. The few that were not had possessed an arrogance that set him on edge. Trying to build a relationship with a Were faced two problems. The first was that he was a Pack Leader, with the obligations that went with the position. Additionally, he was an oddity among Weres in that he had an extended lifespan. If he had taken a fancy to a Were, it would have complicated things within the pack, and he would have lost his mate after what was only a small portion of his life.

He felt a warmth in his heart that he had rarely experienced before in his long, long life. He realized that his life before he met Janna - apart from the all too short love a century ago - had been just marking time. He had causes and people for whom he cared, but after seeing so much of the worst of humanity, he had kept them at arms length with very few exceptions. Paul, Danislav, a handful of others, he had let in close. But none of them as close as the redhead lying next to him.

"I know a way to distract you from your damned introspection," Janna said with mischief in her voice. She rolled over and changed her word to action with a deep, lustful kiss.

They had a late and leisurely breakfast. After eating, Boris sat on the couch, and Janna sat on his lap, kissing him and trying to prod him back to bed. It was not likely that they would have another chance at an uninterrupted weekend for some time. Boris was basking in her affection, and not tempted in the least to move at all. Both were noticeably startled and upset for different reasons when there was an interruption.

Their phone rang. It was set to only let four people ring through. Danislav, Paul, Bethany Anne, and Frank. Janna reached it first.

She looked at the name, clicked the button and started talking, "Frank, what's so important that Boris and I can't get a full weekend alone after nearly two months of combat operations back to back?" she said, unable to keep the irritation entirely of her voice. She was worn to the bone. Everyone else involved, even Danislav, had already had some time off to avoid combat fatigue.

"Hey Janna, I apologize for the interruption, but we have two important items to give you updates about. Would you please put me on the speaker?" There was a pause, as she switched the phone to speaker. "Boris, I figured you would like to know you two didn't end up splitting up Paul's marriage by changing him. While Alecta was not happy, she used the situation first to insist, then argue, then finally ask that she and their sons have the right to choose the same change if they so wished. This was after not talking to Paul for two weeks once he got out of the medipod. Once she was properly respectful, Bethany Anne made sure she understood the risks. She ignored everything she had just been warned about and decided she wanted to be changed as soon as possible." They could hear the amusement in his voice

Boris sighed and said "She was always worried that if he got severely injured on one of our jobs or missions that I'd change him and that afterward, he'd feel she was somehow less. That was just paranoia in my opinion. Paul dotes on that woman."

"I'm more worried about what this will do to our long-time friendship. I am more than his boss. He is my friend. It would grieve me terribly if that changed. I do not want to lose his friendship and our closeness. Besides, this is worse in some ways. Until recently I didn't know I, person-ally, could change people. Previously, Paul would only have been a werewolf. Now he is a werebear, which is not some-thing his wife had ever prepared for or even thought about."

Frank continued, "Bethany Anne agreed that inacti-vating the Pricolici protocols for the nanocytes in Paul was a good idea, so we used his as the base. Their sons are undecided as of yet. Alexi agreed to help the reconciling couple get used to their other forms a few weeks ago. I think he must be one of the few people who likes Paul's sense of humor."

There was a pause on the line, the two of them heard some paper shuffling, "The second thing that you need to know is that you need to get moving. Paul and Alecta will meet you at the location I plan on providing you. We have narrowed down a likely site for the Archangelsk Base. Just give me a time."

Before Boris could answer, Janna said, "We'll get back to you." She quickly killed the call.

"Just one more day Boris?" she asked, a pleading look in her eyes.

"Janna, this is important. We need to find the site. I am not thrilled about having to go to Archangelsk or the region near it. That is the only place that I always got the headaches apart from being near Michael and Barnabas before Bethany Anne fixed me. I can now feel when the Etheric is drawn on but it no longer hurts. Also, my mother told me some family legends about the region that were somewhat terrifying, even when I think of them now. It is said that there was a beast in a cave there from whom our ancestors had fled but…" Boris said

"Wait …headaches?"

"Yes. Terrible headaches, triggered by the Etheric draw of the new technology."

"Give me another day with just us, and I'll tell you of a way that I think we can vastly reduce the time it will take us to find the base."

"Or you could tell me this miraculous method now, and we could find it a day sooner," Boris said in a teasing tone. He knew their time alone together would be cut short as soon as this weekend was over.

Boris, please? she thought to him, the need to continue their time together flowing with her thoughts.

Boris smiled and picked up the phone. He sent a quick

message to Frank and said, "Okay, but we leave at noon tomorrow."

He was almost knocked to the floor by the unexpected and very enthusiastic tackle hug. It was going to be a pleasant and very sweaty day he suspected.

FINIS

Ahh, the second collaboration and the third book is done.

It should be published in 12 hours or so.

At least 30,000 words of this book are my work. I hope people like it. I've been told they will.

I keep getting told that my writing is constantly improving. Personally I can't see the massive improvements people tell me I have in anything but speed. It could be I can't see the forest for the trees.

But my Enjoyment of writing is increasing. I rarely have a day where I don't want to write, where it all seems too hard anymore. Most of this I credit to the fans - Just knowing that my work is getting out there and being appreciated is a big boost. Even if life decides to screw me at least once a week recently.

One of these day's I'm going to find that bloody Murphy and hang him by his toes over hot coals.

But onto the regular theme of my author's notes: How does a Collaboration work in the way that Michael and I are doing it.

Short answer: Well.

Long answer: Communication. I remember early on in the book there was one scene I had to, for all intents, completely re-write because I'd misinterpreted a scene in one of Mike's early books. It was a pain. But the end result worked better.

Running things past Mike at least twice a week helps me make sure I'm on target. If I'm unsure if something fits his universe I drop him a note.

It would be very different if the Universe was shared. Again, and I cannot emphasize this enough, I consider the universe his. I respect that. If there is something he wants changed or scrapped, that is what I do. I think that I now see why some authors explicitly state a 'No Fanfic' rule. It actually makes more sense to me now, than when I was just writing in my own. I can also see why many authors either turn a blind eye or actively (if covertly) encourage it. I'm still on the fence, personally, but in my on series (Betrayed by Faith) I am leaning towards a 'No Fanfic' if only because I will be walking a fine line between condemning some things and disrespecting them. The difference at times, to me, can be a molecule wide.

It is a great privilege to be allowed to write in his universe. I don't think there is much more I can say about that.

Oh and the characters - I'm still not sure where 'Paranoid needle fucker' came from. I think it was Janna reaching out with her unhappiness.

I am really proud of *'**Well doesn't that make us special fucking snowflakes?**'* again, not sure where it came from. It just flowed out onto the keyboard and fit well.

Considering there were at least two people who publicly stated 'Where did Janna come from?' I introduced Shen earlier. He's not much in this book, but he's there and has a larger role to play.

I think we have found our groove, but the next Boris book is probably ten weeks away.

I can hear the mob forming... yup they just lit the torches... Oh, come on, are the tar and feathers *really* necessary?

This is a combination of factors. One of them is that I really need to work on my solo series. No like REALLY. I need to get book two out. It's been 3 months.

The other main factor is - Mike's plot. He has things he wants to happen in his books before the plot of mine takes place. So... Yeah. Sorry.

But Please keep leaving reviews (Yes, your comments were helpful Tesh. A bit out of the blue... well yeah, you want to talk more you have my Facebook :)) The Kind ones encourage. The critical ones help me improve.

Now for those social media links.

This is for my Blog

This is for the Betrayed by Faith Mailing list

This is my Author Facebook

This is the Series Facebook

This is my Amazon Author Page (I'll get around to my Bio one day, I swear!) I try and check it every day. It's a bit quiet though.

P.S. Condemning something is showing disapproval, without inciting to hate. It can include colorful language.

Well, crackers. I don't know what Paul is going to write as I sit here and write this one. So, I can't be snarky and it kinda sucks. I liked the opportunity to know what Paul wrote first last time.

D@mn.

For those that read the author notes in The Kurtherian Gambit series know that I'm new to this author gig. Like, I'm not even out of my Freshman year, yet. So, there is a LOT I haven't seen, witnessed or, sometimes, have a clue about. I just keep taking this authoring gig one day at a time and thank my lucky stars you, the fans, like Bethany Anne and her people.

I try to remember that even 'bad' guys (or females) have reasons they are doing something, usually because we (as parents) screwed something up. Well, at least that is how it feels sometimes. Mind you, occasionally the parents deserve it, sometimes not. Either way, once they are outside of the family walls, it is all on them to stand up and be accountable for their actions.

So Paul had intended to write a different book first before tackling this one. The problem, as he told me, was this story was in his head so much, he couldn't focus on his other book. So, he needed to get this story out, and he did.

Really, really quickly. I'm writing this Author note about 29 days from the last author note on July 14th.

With the awesome fan base for The Kurtherian Gambit, and a strong spin-off character in Boris, the first book, Evacuation, STAYED #1 in its category for a looooong time. In fact, due to the first book, I had two (2) #1 books in their genre at one time (TKG 11 - Sued for Peace and The Boris Chronicles, Evacuation). Evacuation is still #3 in the Best Sellers in Action & Adventure Short Stories right next to #2 by George R. R. Martin himself.

Pretty cool.

Now, we are releasing Retaliation and we intend (for at least a few days) to knock ol' George off his throne.

Maybe...I hope. ;-)

If we do, it will be a really cool feeling, I have to say.

Forever grateful for my family, my readers and fans, our beta-readers and our editor in all things.

Michael Anderle

Mongrelverse Series

Breed Matters

- Book 1 – A Mongrel's Curse
- Book 2 – Mongrel's Tooth and Consequence (2nd Quarter 2017)

Face The Music

- Book 1 – WereEagles Fear to Tread
- Book 2 – A Mongrel, A Bard and Witches, Oh My!

Mother of Monsters

- Book 1 – Cursed Mother (1st Quarter 2017)
- Book 2 – Forsaking Motherhood (2nd Quarter 2017)
- Book 3 – Mother Remade (2nd Quarter 2017)

Misc. Shorts

- A Simple Trip
- Guarding An Imp (published in Flight of the Phoenix Anthology)

Betrayed by Faith

- Book 1 – Paladin
- Book 2 - A-Viking
- Book 3 – Myrmidon (3rd Quarter 2017)

The Boris Chronicles (Kurtherian Universe, With Michael Anderle)

- Book 1 – Evacuation
- Book 2 - Retaliation
- Book 3 - Revelations
- Book 4 – Title pending (2nd Quarter 2017)

Short Story Contributions to Anthologies

- Inanna's Circle Game, Volume 4 (edited by Kat Lind)
- The Expanding Universe, Volume 1 (edited by Craig Martelle)

These can be found and will be published on Paul C Middleton's Author page.

WANT MORE PAUL C MIDDLETON?

Join Paul's Email List here: http://eepurl.com/bZxFvD

Join Paul's Facebook Group Here: https://www. facebook.com/Betrayed-by-Faith-1110766018944080/

WANT MORE FROM LMBPN PUBLISHING?

Website:
http://www.lmbpn.com

Email List:
http://lmbpn.com/email/

Join the Kurtherian Gambit Facebook Group Here:
https://www.facebook.com/TheKurtherianGambitBooks/